Favourite
Ballet Stories

Chosen by

DARCEY BUSSELL

RED FOX

FAVOURITE BALLET STORIES
A RED FOX BOOK 0 099 417596

First published in Great Britain by Red Fox,
an imprint of Random House Children's Books

This edition published 2002

7 9 10 8 6

Papers used by Random House Children's Books are natural, recyclable products made
from wood grown in sustainable forests. The manufacturing processes conform to the
environmental regulations of the country of origin.

Set in Guardi

Red Fox Books are published by Random House Children's Books,
61–63 Uxbridge Road, London W5 5SA,
a division of The Random House Group Ltd,
in Australia by Random House Australia (Pty) Ltd
20 Alfred Street, Milsons Point, Sydney, NSW 2061, Australia,
in New Zealand by Random House New Zealand Ltd,
18 Poland Road, Glenfield, Auckland 10, New Zealand,
and in South Africa by Random House South Africa (Pty) Ltd,
Endulini, 5A Jubilee Road, Parktown 2193, South Africa

TTHE RANDOM HOUSE GROUP Limited Reg. No. 954009
www.kidsatrandomhouse.co.uk

A CIP catalogue for this book is available from the British Library.

Printed and bound in Great Britain by Cox & Wyman Ltd, Reading, Berkshire

Contents

Introduction

I'm not sure of my earliest memory of ballet dancing; it may have been the playing of some notes on a piano, or the fiddling with the chiffon of my skirt, or dancing in the kitchen at home. But I do remember, exactly, how much I enjoyed reading a well-written story of the theatre or ballet when I was young and how they caught my imagination and often inspired me.

Now, I thought I would tell you my own story, about the day I first wore pointe shoes. I remember it as clearly as if it were yesterday. I was lucky enough to be attending an early Saturday morning ballet class with my friends at the Mercury Theatre in Notting Hill Gate, then home of the Ballet Rambert. I was about ten years old, and I recall sitting on the floor putting a white animal's wool in my first ever pair of pointe shoes. They smelt so new and special, a canvas and leather smell. The shoes looked very beautiful, too, with their pale-pink satin outside, and they looked so delicate. I was terribly excited and so were my friends and we gingerly eased our feet into them. Our teacher instructed us on how to wrap our ribbons around our ankles. I stood on pointe and it hurt a lot! I clutched on to the barre for support and wobbled like a young deer standing for the first time. I didn't think it was going to be as hard as this. I so wanted it to look as easy as the pictures of the famous dancers in their grand poses. However, as I looked at my feet in the mirror, I thought I saw a glimpse of how a professional ballerina looked. I loved that idea! If only I'd known of all the hard work to come. That moment was magical for me and I shall remember it for the rest of my life.

Theatre life has its ups and downs, but I enjoy the hard work and discipline required to make any theatre company successful. The stage is always full of drama, passion and challenges and as a result exciting performances always occur.

Many of the stories in this collection reflect the first impressions of young people being exposed to this different world and tell of an important moment in a young person's discovery of dance, and some accurately reflect my own experiences, such as my first visit to the Royal Opera House when I was a student at White Lodge, the Royal Ballet School. I really do hope you enjoy them.

Darcey Bussell

I Don't Want
to Dance!

by Bel Mooney

Kitty's cousin Melissa had started ballet classes.

'Why don't you go as well, dear?' suggested Kitty's mum.

'I don't want to dance!' growled Kitty, picking up her biro to draw a skull and crossbones on her hand. Mum sighed, looking at Kitty's tousled hair, dirty nails, and the dungarees all covered in soil – from where Kitty had been playing Crawling Space Creatures with William from next door.

'I think it would be nice for you,' she said, 'because you'd learn … you'd learn … Well, dancing makes you strong.'

'No,' said Kitty – and that was that.

But when Kitty's big brother Daniel came home from school and heard about the plan, he laughed. 'Kitty go to ballet!' he screamed. 'That's a joke! She'd dance like a herd of elephants!'

Just then Dad came in, and smiled. 'Well, I think she'd dance like Muhammad Ali.'

'Who's he?' Kitty asked.

'He was a boxer,' grinned Dad.

That did it. If there was one thing Kitty hated it was being teased (although to tell the truth she didn't mind teasing other people!). 'Right! I'll show you!' she yelled.

So on Saturday afternoon Kitty was waiting outside the hall with the other girls (and two boys) from the ballet class. Mum had taken her shopping that morning, and Kitty had chosen a black leotard, black tights and black ballet shoes. Now she saw that all the other girls were in pink. She felt like an ink blot.

Mum went off for coffee with Auntie Susan, leaving Kitty with Melissa and her friend, Emily. They both had their hair done up in a bun, and wore little short net skirts over their leotards. They looked Kitty up and down in a very snooty way.

'You could never be a ballet dancer, Kitty, 'cos you're too clumsy,' said Melissa.

'And you're too small,' said Emily.

Kitty glared at them. 'I don't want to dance anyway,' she said. 'I'm only coming to this boring old class to please Mum.'

But she felt horrid inside, and she wished – oh, how she wished – she was playing in the garden with William. Pirates. Explorers. Cowboys. Crawling Space Creatures. Those were the games they played and Kitty knew they suited her more than ballet class.

She put both hands up to her head and tore out the neat bunches Mum had insisted on. That's better

– that's more like *me*, she thought.

Miss Francis, the ballet teacher, was very pretty and graceful, with long black hair in a knot on top of her head. She welcomed Kitty and asked if she had done ballet before.

'No,' said Kitty in a small, sulky voice.

'Never mind,' said Miss Francis. 'You'll soon catch up with the others. Stand in front of me and watch my feet. Now, class, make rows ... heels together ... First position!'

Kitty put her heels together, and tried to put her feet in a straight line, like Miss Francis. But it was very hard. She bent her knees – that made it easier.

There was a giggle from behind.

'Look at Kitty,' whispered Emily. 'She looks like a duck!'

Miss Francis didn't hear. 'Good!' she called. 'Now, do you all remember the first position for your arms? Let's see if we can put it all together ...'

Kitty looked at the girls each side of her, then at Miss Francis – and put her arms in the air. She stretched up, but was thinking so hard about her arms she forgot what her feet were doing. Then she thought about her feet, and forgot to look up at her arms.

There was an explosion of giggles from behind.

'Kitty looks like a tree in a storm,' whispered Melissa.

'Or like a drowning duck!' said Emily.

'Shh, girls!' called Miss Francis with a frown.

And so it went on. Kitty struggled to copy all the

9

positions, but she was always a little bit behind. Once, when Miss Francis went over to speak to the lady playing the piano, she turned round quickly and stuck her tongue out at Melissa and Emily.

Of course, that only made them giggle more. And some of the other children joined in. It wasn't that they wanted to be mean to Kitty – not really. It was just that she looked so funny, with her terrible frown, and her hair sticking out all over the place. And they thought she felt she was better than all of them. But of course the truth was that the horrible feeling inside Kitty was growing so fast she was afraid it would burst out of her eyes.

Everybody seemed so clever and skilful – except her.

'I *am* an ink blot,' she thought miserably.

It so happened that Miss Francis was much more than pretty and graceful; she was a very good teacher. She saw Kitty's face and heard the giggles, and knew exactly what was going on. So she clapped her hands and told all the children to sit in a circle.

'Now, we're going to do some free dancing,' she said, 'so I want some ideas from you all. What could we all be …?'

Lots of hands shot up, because the class enjoyed this. 'Let's do a flower dance,' called Melissa.

'Birds,' suggested Emily.

'Let's pretend we're trees … and the hurricane comes,' called out one of the boys.

'I want to be a flower,' Melissa insisted.

Miss Francis looked at Kitty. 'What about you? You haven't said anything,' she said with a smile.

Kitty shook her head.

'Come on, Kitty, I know you must have an idea. Tell me what we can be when we dance. Just say whatever comes into your head.'

'Crawling Space Creatures,' said Kitty.

The children began to laugh. But Miss Francis held up her hand. 'What a good idea! Tell us a little bit about them first, so we can imagine them …'

'Well, me and William play it in the garden, and we live on this planet which is all covered with jungle, and we're really horrible-looking things, with no legs, just tentacles like octopuses. And so we move about by crawling, but since we like the food that grows at the top of the bushes we sometimes have to rear up, and that's very hard, see. And we have to be careful, 'cos there's these birds that eat us if they see us, so we have to keep down. Sometimes William is the birds, and tries to get me …'

'All right, children – you're all Crawling Space Creatures. We'll see if we can get some spooky, space-like music on the piano …'

The lady playing the piano smiled and nodded.

So they began. Most of the children loved the idea, but Melissa and Emily and two other girls looked very cross and bored.

'Down on the floor, girls!' called Miss Francis.

Kitty had a wonderful time. She listened to the music, and imagined the strange planet, and twisted her body into all sorts of fantastic shapes. After a few minutes Miss Francis told the others to stop. 'All watch Kitty!' she said.

So the children made a circle, and Kitty did her own dance. She lay on the floor and twisted and turned, waving her arms in time to the music.

Sometimes she would crouch, then rear up, as if reaching for strange fruit, only to duck down in terror, waving her 'tentacles', as the savage birds wheeled overhead ...

At last the music stopped, and all the children clapped. Kitty looked up shyly. She had forgotten where she was. She had lost herself in her dance.

When the lesson was over, Miss Francis beckoned Kitty to come over to the piano. None of the children noticed; they were all crowding round the door to meet their mothers.

'Now, Kitty,' said Miss Francis quietly, 'what do you think you've learned about ballet today?'

'It's hard,' said Kitty.

'Well, yes, it is hard. But what else? What about your space dance?'

'That was fun!'

'Because it was *you*?'

Kitty nodded.

'Well, we'll do lots of made-up dances too, and you'll find you can be lots of things – if you let yourself. That's what modern ballet is all about, you know. Now take this book, and look at the pictures, and you can practise all the positions for next week ... You are coming next week?'

Kitty nodded happily, and went off to find Mum. Outside in the hall Melissa and Emily glared at her.

'Look at my tights – they're all dirty,' moaned Melissa.

'All that crawling about on the floor – so babyish!' said Emily, in the snootiest voice.

'If you knew anything, you'd know that's what modern ballet is all about,' said Kitty, in her most wise and grown-up voice. 'I shall have to teach you some more about it next week. Now, if you'll just let me past, I'm going to go home and practise.'

Mr George

by Jamila Gavin

He heard music in the night. Distant music, from far, far away; but its energy made his body twitch. Lying in bed, Kit's feet wriggled, his muscles flexed. The rhythms of the music seemed to enter his bloodstream and course round his body, lifting him from his bed. He sprang right into the middle of the floor.

How strange. There was a trap door there in the middle of his bedroom floor. He had never noticed it before, and from somewhere beneath the trap door, somewhere beneath his wriggling feet, came the music. It was irresistible. Kit tugged a brass ring and lifted open the trap door. The music flooded out. Hastily, he climbed down the steps, pulling the door down over his head, lest the sound should waken everybody.

At the bottom of the steps, he paused and breathed deeply. He stood in the wings of a vast stage. He felt as nervous as if he were about to walk out and perform before hundreds of people, all waiting somewhere in the darkness, beyond the row of footlights which dazzled him.

The stage was set like a wood – but a wood made entirely of crystal. The trees were white and glistening – their trunks, shards of glass, their twigs were icicles and their leaves like droplets of dew.

Somewhere below the stage in the pit, an orchestra played music: violins and cellos, oboes and flutes – sadly, merrily, energetically, hauntingly – it made him want to dance.

A figure appeared and disappeared as she wound her way through the trees. Like a ballerina or a sylph, she was white and fluttery. Sometimes she was just one figure, but other times, her reflection was multiplied over and over in the trembling crystals. He must follow. He stepped on to the stage. His tread made the crystal wood tinkle and flash with all the colours of the rainbow. In time with the clash of a cymbal, he leapt forward and almost reached the ballerina, but then there was a thundering of drums and everything went dark. The crystal wood vanished, and he found himself lying on the floor back in his bedroom.

He crawled over to his bedside table and switched on the lamp. His heart thudded. He pulled back the carpet and felt a wave of disappointment. No, he hadn't been awake. It wasn't real. There were only the bare boards. No trap door. No crystal wood and fleeting sylph. He had been dreaming those dreams again, those wide awake dreams which seemed so real.

Yet – there was music. It was very faint, but he could hear it and he wasn't asleep now. It came not from below, but from somewhere above his head.

Kit stared up at the ceiling wonderingly. The little chandelier, which his mother had found in a junk shop, and insisted on hanging in his room, was swaying and tinkling.

Mr George lived in the flat above, and he often played music. But who could be moving around and making his chandelier tinkle? Not Mr George; he had become almost housebound with arthritis. His carer had long since put him to bed and gone, yet Kit was sure he could make out a faint pattering of something moving across the ceiling above him, something which made the chandelier sway. The music lilted and waltzed, and the little droplets of crystals gently shimmered. Like one hypnotized, he fell back into his bed with drooping eyelids, and slept.

He would have forgotten all about it, except he found his bedside light on the next morning, and remembered. He glanced up. The chandelier was absolutely still now. He checked his watch. In five minutes, Mr George's carer would come to wash and dress the old man, and help him into his wheelchair in the window, from where he could view the world coming and going.

Some days later, a letter was wrongly delivered to their flat. It was addressed to Mr Ivan George. 'Kit! Just pop this letter upstairs to Mr George!' cried his mother.

When Kit reached the top of the red-carpeted stairs and stood before Mr George's door he heard the music. It was the same music he had heard the other night in his dream. He stood spellbound, feeling his muscles twitch and his toes wriggle. At last he knocked, feeling suddenly shy. He had never been in Mr George's flat before.

'Enter!' an oddly high voice, with a strange accent called out to him. He turned the knob. The door was unlocked, and he walked in. It was as if he had walked on stage before curtain up, for before him was a heavy, deep crimson, velvet curtain which created a dark lobby before entering the apartment.

Nervously, he peeped round the curtain. 'Er … Mr George?'

This time, there was no answer, but the music flowed around him. Kit stepped into the apartment. 'Mr George?' he called again. What a strange room it was. There was hardly any furniture to speak of; a straight-backed chair, a small table and an upright piano. There were no carpets on the floor, just bare boards looking worn and scratched from wear. It must be easier for a wheelchair, thought Kit. Faded red velvet curtains hung in the bay window, held back by shabby gold tassels and, at the far end of the room, a huge mirror, full of dark, trembling reflections, stretched from ceiling to floor.

But what really captured his eye were the photographs all round the walls. They were old, black and white photographs, all of dancers: some were beautiful ballerinas in stiff sticky-out tutus like daisies or candy tuft, others looked like swans in their flowing long dresses. Many of the photographs were of hunters and warriors – muscular and strong – spinning high into the air, or leaping like tigers across a stage.

One photograph in particular captured Kit's eye. It was of a dancer dressed in the costume of a prince. He wore a swirling cloak and hunting boots, and held a bow in one hand while, on his other arm, he supported a ballerina. As delicate as a snowdrop, in a long, white, flowing ballet dress, the ballerina drooped in his arms, balanced on the pointe of one foot, while her other leg extended upwards like a swan.

The prince stared out of the photograph; a proud young man with dark hooded eyes, high cheekbones, and a mass of unruly black curls, and he seemed to be boasting, 'I am the best in the world.'

He must have been famous, for some of the photographs were of him with famous people – and one even showed him bowing before the Queen.

Then Kit saw Mr George. He was in his wheelchair in the bay window, half hidden by the curtain, his head bowed down on to his chest and his eyes closed.

'Mr George?' Kit whispered nervously.

The old man looked up, nodding slowly. 'Come, come!' he said in that strange voice.

'I, er ...' Kit held out the letter. 'This is yours,' he said. 'It came to us by mistake.' He went up to him tentatively.

Mr George took the envelope with a quivering hand. However, the look he gave Kit was not old and bleary, but suddenly awake, sharp and scrutinizing.

'Where are you from, boy?' he asked. 'Do I know you?'

'Yes, sir, I mean, no, sir. I mean, I live downstairs.'

'Ah yes, downstairs!' The old man looked at the letter in his hand and his thoughts seemed to drift away. Kit backed towards the door behind the curtain. 'Goodbye,' he said and quickly left.

It was some time before Kit had the dream again – but when it came, it was just as powerful as before. A dream so real, he thought he was awake.

He heard music. Music which made him want to go on stage and hop and leap and skip. He leapt from his bed and crawled about on the floor looking for the trap door, but it wasn't there. He shivered. He was awake. Kit reached for the bedside light. This was no dream. The music was real, and it came from upstairs. He looked up at his chandelier. It was trembling, and now he was sure he could hear other bumps and thumps and creaking sounds. Perhaps Mr George had fallen and was trying to get help.

Bare-footed, he crept to his door and opened it. A dim night-light glimmered in the hallway. The red-carpeted stairway rose into the shadows above. Step by step, he climbed and reached Mr George's door. He stood there, listening, wondering if he should knock. He raised a hand, but saw the door was open. He saw a light and stepped inside the lobby. He peeped round the curtain and almost cried out loud with shock.

It was his dream. There was the huge stage with the row of dazzling footlights; a black void swept out over the pit where an orchestra played, and out into the dark auditorium packed with rows of people. He could just see their rows of heads, and caught the glimmerings of hundreds of eyes.

The stage was set, as in his dream, like a crystal wood.

Through the great mirror at the back of the room Mr George's flat was reflected, shimmering with crystals, white and flashing with rainbow colours from glass twigs and branches which criss-crossed the room. It seemed to stretch on and on to a shining lake in the distance.

On the edge of the lake he saw the ballerina, a sylph all in white, swirling as she danced. A prince sped after her down the path. It was the prince in the photograph, with billowing cloak, leather hunting boots and bow in hand.

The music in the pit below the stage grew louder; its rhythms made Kit's feet flex and tap in time. He wanted to join in. The prince reached the sylph, flung off his cloak, then, as if to show off in front of her, began to dance. His dance was proud; his dance was wild. He leapt high and clicked his heels, he sprang round her like a stallion, twirling and spinning, yet never losing his balance, and when he had finished, he bowed before her and kissed her hand. She laughed and clapped – but then suddenly, the ballerina saw Kit.

Her eyes widened as they stared into his. She pointed at him. The prince turned, his hand on his dagger, and began to advance towards him.

Kit had the strangest feeling that with every step,

the young prince grew older and older, and more and more hunched and twisted. He shook his head as if in despair and stretched out a hand. Panic-stricken, Kit let drop the curtain and backed out of the door. He fled down the stairs two and three at a time, and flung himself, panting, into bed.

The chandelier was swaying furiously, but the sound had ceased. Kit lay back, his heart still thudding. He watched the chandelier till it finally stopped trembling, and hung still and frozen. It was nearly dawn before he slept.

The next morning, Kit was woken by a commotion. The sound of a vehicle drawing up; voices in the hallway. The chandelier above his head swayed vigorously as several feet pounded to and fro.

'What's going on?' Kit went into the hall and looked up the stairwell to Mr George's flat. Then he saw the stretcher being carried out by two men in uniform. Kit sprang up the stairs. 'Are you ill, Mr George?' he cried with alarm. The two men tried to keep him back, but Kit bent over the old man, who lay there with his eyes shut.

'Mr George?' Kit whispered.

The old man opened his eyes. His lips moved. He wanted to say something. Kit bent lower to hear.

'Go to the wood,' Mr George said in a voice so soft Kit had to bend even closer. 'She's waiting. You'll have to take my place. You will go, won't you?'

Then the ambulance men whisked him away.

That night he heard the dancing music. He sat up in the darkness, wide awake. He didn't leap into the centre of his bedroom and look for the trap door. He knew the music was coming from Mr George's flat upstairs. He slipped out of bed and out into the hall. He climbed the red-carpeted stairs till he reached the first floor and stood before Mr George's door.

Surely it would be locked? He tried the handle. The door swung open.

He stood behind the thick velvet curtains. He could hear the music coming from a great distance. With trembling hand, he pulled aside the curtain. But he was surprised; disappointed even. There was no stage, no crystal wood. Mr George's flat was just as it was before, with its bare floorboards, one chair and table and one upright piano; and, of course, the photographs of dancers and ballerinas round the room.

But where was the one of the prince holding the beautiful drooping sylph? Strange. There was a picture of a sylph, who arched forward on one leg into a deep arabesque, while her other leg stretched out beneath her long flowing white dress – but she was alone. The handsome, haughty prince who had supported her had gone.

The music got louder. The harp strings echoed with a long trickling glissando. The ballerina in the photograph spun round and stepped out of the picture frame and, as she did, the whole room was transformed into the crystal wood.

The ballerina was looking for someone. She ran

here and there through the trees, looking everywhere. She ran to the edge of the stage and looked out into the black void beyond the footlights. Where was the prince?

Kit looked at the photograph. It was a blank. The frame was empty.

The ballerina returned towards him, her arms outstretched. 'Dance with me,' she pleaded with her dark eyes. He took her hand – and suddenly, he was dancing.

◉

At breakfast, the next morning, Kit's mother glanced through the newspaper, before bundling all of them into the car to get to school and on to work. 'Oh!' she said with a sad sigh.

'What?' asked Kit.

'Ivan Gregorski died yesterday. He was very old. He used to be my pin-up when I was a young girl! He was a wonderful dancer. I used to dream of being a ballerina. I wanted to grow up and dance with Ivan Gregorski.'

Kit looked at the photograph. It showed a young man, with a haughty, regal look. He had glowering eyes and a broad brow, an unsmiling mouth and a narrow long nose. His hair was dark, and unruly with curls ... and he seemed to be saying, 'I am the greatest!'

It was Mr George.

◉

That night, Kit awoke to the sound of music. He looked up at his chandelier. It trembled as if a wind blew through its crystals. Upstairs, he knew the ballerina was waiting for someone to dance with her. 'Take my place,' old Mr George had begged.

Kit leapt from his bed, the music making his feet twitch and his muscles flex. 'Yes! Ivan Gregorski,' he whispered. 'Yes. I'll take your place.'

Mega-Nuisance

by Geraldine Kaye

'Paddy, you should shut your mouth when you're eating,' Rosalind said crossly. 'I don't want to see all your chewed-up liver and bacon, thanks very much.'

'You know he finds it difficult, Rozzy,' Mum said gently. 'Especially now with this awful cold and his nose stuffed up, poor little chap.'

Rosalind said nothing. A seven-year-old brother like Paddy who was all hugs and kisses, *who needed it?* she thought.

'Your audition tomorrow, isn't it?' Daddy said as if her bad mood needed explaining. 'Don't let it get to you, poppet. It's not the end of the world if you don't get in.'

'I know,' Rosalind said out loud but secretly she thought it *would* be the end of the world. She had been thinking about the audition, working towards it, ever since she had done her first ballet exam and Miss Reid had put her into the acceleration class for gifted pupils. In October she had got through the preliminary audition for entrance to White Lodge, the Royal Ballet School at Richmond. Now it was

February and tomorrow was the *final* audition. They lived too far away for daily travel. She would have to board and the best thing about that was she would only have to put up with Paddy at half-term and holidays. If she got into White Lodge.

'Wozzy?' Paddy said, smiling widely as Mum wiped his face and hands and let him get down from his chair. He couldn't say his 'r's properly. 'Wozzy?' He was beside her now, pulling at her skirt and staring up at her with his eyes like grey marbles. 'Wozzy wead …? Wozzy wead …?'

'Sorry,' Rosalind said getting up. She kicked off her shoes and gripped the back of her chair and raised one leg to illustrate. 'I'm busy, Paddy. I've got to do a barre tonight.' She had to see to her pointes and her ribbons and practise her *pliés* but you couldn't explain things like that to Paddy.

Miss Reid had said her *pliés* could let down her whole *enchaînement*. Even the greatest dancers had stronger and weaker parts to their dancing, Miss Reid said.

'Wozzy wead …? Wozzy wead …?' Paddy said batting the book against her.

'Oh, read to him for a minute while we wash up, there's a love,' Mum said. 'You're his favourite person, you know.'

'Big deal,' Rosalind said. He certainly wasn't hers and she couldn't pretend. She wasn't good at pretending.

'Wozzy wead …?'

'Oh, all right, mega-nuisance,' Rosalind said,

walking off to the sitting room. 'Bring your book then.'

How could you be fond of somebody you don't like looking at? she wondered as he scrambled on to her lap and put his arms lovingly round her neck. A long time ago, alone in the sitting room with Paddy, she had held his lips closed between her fingers as if she could change him. Perhaps Paddy had wanted her to change him too because he hadn't pulled away. He just stared at her with tears running down his face.

He had been four then. She had been four when he was born. 'Why is he so ugly?' she had said, seeing him at the hospital for the first time. She was too young to know it was better not to say things like that. 'Poor little chap, poor little boy,' Mum had said, rocking him tenderly. Had she ever held her like that when she was a baby? Rosalind wondered.

Afterwards, Daddy had explained that Paddy was a Down's syndrome child, some people called it mongol. He would always have some trouble learning to do things, but he should be able to go to school and learn to read and write. Later he might get a job doing simple work. He was delicate too: he had cold after cold. His heart was damaged and his lungs didn't work properly. They would all have to work hard helping Paddy to learn to keep his tongue in and his mouth closed. Daddy said there were many things Paddy would do very well, but he might take a long time to learn.

Rosalind tried hard to be nice to Paddy like

Mum was. But it was just too difficult. How could she bring friends home, for instance, with him in the house? Once she had heard girls in the cloakroom whispering, 'Have you seen her brother? Well, he's funny.'

'He's not funny,' she had shouted, erupting through the thicket of coats like an avenging angel. 'He's Down's syndrome, so there.'

They had all gone pink and Tracey's mouth fell open like a parody of Paddy's. Well, it would all be different if she got into White Lodge. All her form were going to Hill Street Comprehensive next year and she need never see any of them again. And nobody from White Lodge need ever see Paddy, if she didn't want them to.

'Wead us ... wead us ...' Paddy had opened the book and was snuggling against her. His fair hair still smelled of liver and bacon.

His favourite story was *The Tin Soldier* by Hans Andersen and that was odd because it had been her favourite story too. The tin soldier was disabled with only one leg, she supposed, but he stood straight and true whatever happened, even when he was swallowed by a big fish. The tin soldier loved the paper dancer, and no wonder, Rosalind thought, she loved her too. The little dancer who stood on the mantelpiece was partly herself of course. But why did Paddy love the story? He wasn't anything like the tin soldier who stood true and steadfast whatever happened, or anybody else in the story unless it was the fish with the big swallowing mouth.

Still it was the story he always wanted read. Not that she really had to read it because she knew it by heart. She recited her way through while Mum and Daddy cleared the table.

'Goodnight, mega-nuisance,' she said as Daddy gave Paddy a piggyback upstairs to bed. They were both so good with Paddy, made such a fuss of him. Once she had tried to say something about it and Mum had said, 'Well, of course ... they didn't think he'd survive ... I mean we're lucky to have him ... we have to make the most of him while ... because ...' She never finished the sentence, just blinked and added, 'Oh, sorry, Rozzy dear ...' But it was clear what she meant.

That evening Rosalind darned the toes of her pointes with pink silk more carefully than she had ever done before. Everything was ready for the next day but the night was full of restless, anxious dreams. Saturday morning was sunny, the sky a comforting Cambridge blue as Rosalind got dressed. Mum was going to drive her to Richmond.

'Car?' said Paddy, running to the door after breakfast. 'Me come in car?'

'You're not taking him?' Rosalind said.

'Well, he does love the car so,' Mum said apologetically. 'Daddy's going to take him to Richmond Park to see the deer while you're having your audition.'

'No,' said Rosalind. Somebody might see him and nobody from White Lodge was ever going to see Paddy. 'I'm not going then.' She sat down in the chair in the hall. 'If you're taking Paddy, I'm not going.'

There was a pause. Daddy and Mum looked at each other and then Daddy said, 'Tell you what, we'll go to the park here, Paddy, eh? Feed the ducks.'

'Park with Wozzy ...?' Paddy said looking from one face to the other uncertainly.

'Better get going, you two,' Daddy said crisply. 'Good luck, poppet, I'm sure you'll do fine.'

'Thanks,' said Rosalind. They set off. It was a two-hour journey and Mum didn't say a word, but her lips pressed together said a silent *selfish*. And Rosalind couldn't get Paddy's disappointed face out of her head, which was really unfair, she thought, because she *ought* to be thinking about her *pliés* which Miss Reid said was the one thing which might let her down.

She never really knew what happened. All she heard was a screech of brakes and then a stupendous crash and a jerk which flung her against her seat belt, then the side of the Mini caved in like toffee. A shower of glass and then blackness.

She woke up in hospital. Daddy was there and her leg was hurting badly and so was her head.

'What happened? Where's Mum?'

'Don't worry, love. She's quite all right. She's at home with Paddy. Nothing but a few bruises. It was you who copped it, you've broken your leg.'

'What ...?' It was dark outside. 'What time is it?'

'About seven o'clock.'

'The audition ...?'

'I'm afraid it was all over long ago,' Daddy said.

'Did I … didn't I …?' She still didn't know what had happened. She didn't know anything except there was this terrible pain in her leg. And thousands of bandages.

'The car was hit by a lorry,' Daddy explained, taking her hand. 'You've been concussed. Your leg was badly broken. They had to put a pin in it, bit of metal or plastic or something. But the doctor thinks you'll be quite all right eventually. Probably not even a limp.'

'Eventually?' Rosalind whispered. How long was eventually?

She stared at the pale grey walls of the women's surgical ward. Everybody said she was very brave. At first the woman in the next bed tried to talk but Rosalind turned away. For a bit she wondered if she could have an audition later, next year say, they took people at twelve, didn't they? But then Miss Reid came to see her and she shook her head. 'Such a shame, this setback,' she said, but a lifetime of teaching ballet had accustomed her to setbacks. She smiled at Rosalind kindly. 'I daresay you'll be able to go on with your grades later on,' she said vaguely. She didn't come again.

Daddy or Mum came every day. They brought books and puzzles and things to do but Rosalind took no interest. She had no interest in anything. Going to White Lodge had been the first step to a ballet career and if she couldn't take even the first step, she didn't want to take any step at all.

'You're not dying, you know,' the physiotherapist said quite irritably one day. 'You really must try to work at your exercises or you won't improve.'

'I don't care,' Rosalind said. She couldn't pre tend. She had never been good at pretending.

One afternoon Tracey and Holly came from Grove Road Primary. The top class had drawn get-well cards. Nearly all of them had a ballet girl standing on her pointes.

'Thanks,' Rosalind said and her eyes filled with tears.

'I don't suppose you'll be going to that school, will you, that posh ballet school? I mean it's great, you'll be coming to Hill Street Comprehensive with the rest of us, eh?' Tracey said, trying to be nice. Rosalind just stared at them with tears streaming down her face until a nurse led them away. 'It's no good being sorry for ourselves,' the same nurse said later that evening. 'You're lucky to be alive, young lady.' Rosalind had stopped crying then. She put the ballet girl cards under her pillow.

'How's Paddy?' she said when Mum came that evening.

'He's all right. Well, he's got a bit of a cold as a matter of fact and a chesty cough. Doctor's put him on antibiotics and he's got to stay in bed. Still he's a good little patient. He talks about you all the time. He'd got Granny reading him *The Tin Soldier* when I left. Nothing ever seems to get him down … so brave … marvellous really.'

'Mm,' said Rosalind. At first she was glad not to

be there, listening to Paddy coughing in the next room. But that night she woke and looked at the moon shining pale through the curtains and she wondered if he was all right.

'Why don't you bring Paddy to see me?' she said that next day. She was sitting in a chair by this time.

'Well ... we didn't think you ...'

'I'd *really* like to see him,' she said. 'I mean it's been ages.'

'Well, when he's better ... He's still got a temperature, you know.' Mum looked worried when she spoke but Rosalind didn't realize how worried until after she had gone. That night she woke and, lying in the ward with quiet breathing all round her, she was sure that something awful was happening to Paddy. And the more she thought about it the more she was sure that he was really sick. Paddy who loved her most in the world was really ill and she might never see him again and they weren't telling her ... just making excuses ...

'Where's Paddy?' she said quite loudly when Daddy came next day and several heads turned to look. 'Why didn't you bring him?'

'Paddy? He's all right,' Daddy said. 'He's outside as a matter of fact. Mum thought they'd better wait in the car. Well, his temperature's down but he's still got a bit of a cold.'

'I want to see him,' Rosalind almost shouted.

'Well, OK, poppet,' Daddy said. 'No need to get all het up.' He waved from the window, beckoning.

She could see at once that Paddy was all right

when he came running into the ward.

'Wozzy … Wozzy … Wozzy,' he shouted, scrambling joyfully on to the bed and hugging her, anointing her cheek with two weeks' supply of wet kisses. He was just the same, grey eyes, blond hair. 'Wozzy wead … Wozzy wead book.'

'Oh, all right, mega-nuisance,' she said and Paddy grinned hugely at the familiar word. The book fell open at the right page and she began to recite. The woman in the next bed was smiling, whispering to Mum, 'Ever so good with him, isn't she?'

She was like the paper dancer, Rosalind thought, listening to the sound of her own voice, the paper dancer who had been burned up in the fire. That was right. But Paddy wasn't like the big-mouthed fish at all. He was like the tin soldier who stood brave and true on his one leg and went on loving the paper dancer whatever happened.

Paddy *was* the tin soldier, steadfast to the end.

Hi There, Supermouse

by Jean Ure

*Nicola's parents have always told her she's no good at
dancing, unlike her sister Rose, who is considered a
rising star. Then one day Nicola meets Mrs French,
who thinks she has real talent and offers her a part in
a play. Rose is mortified and, before Nicola realizes
what is happening, she takes her part. But Mrs
French has other ideas ...*

It was half-past nine when Mrs French dropped
Nicola off in Fenning Road.

'Don't forget,' she said. 'Tell Rose we definitely
still want her.'

'Yes. All right.' Nicola, in her eagerness, was
already through the gate and halfway up the path. 'I'll
tell her.'

She hopped up the step into the front porch and
jabbed her finger on the bell, keeping it pressed there
till someone should come.

'What's all the panic?' It was her father who
eventually opened the door. 'Don't tell me they've

landed at last?'

'Who?' Nicola paused impatiently, already poised for flight.

'The little green men,' said Mr Bruce.

'Oh!' She didn't have time, just now, for her father's jokes; she had news to break. She tore across the hall and into the sitting room. 'Mrs French wants me to –'

The words died on her lips: Rose was there, curled up in pyjamas and dressing gown on the sofa. She had obviously been allowed to come downstairs and watch television to make up for having missed the rehearsal.

'Mrs French wants you to what?'

Her mother twisted round to look at her. Nicola stood awkwardly on one leg in the doorway. Somehow, with Rose there, all triumph had gone.

'She wants me to –'

'Well?'

'She wants me to do the part –'

She tried not to look at Rose as she said it, but her eyes *would* go sliding over, just for a quick glance. A quick glance was enough: Rose's pink cheeks had turned bright scarlet, her freckles standing out like splotches of brown paint carelessly flicked off the end of a paint brush. Nicola forced herself to look at something else. It seemed too much like spying, to look at Rose.

Mr Bruce came back in, closing the door behind him. He gave Nicola a little push.

'Born in a field?'

40

Nicola didn't say anything. He was always saying 'Born in a field?' when she didn't close doors behind her. Mrs Bruce, leaning forward to see round her husband as he crossed back to his armchair, said, 'What do you mean, she wants you to do the part?'

'She wants me to do it – instead of Rose. But it's all right,' said Nicola. 'She still wants Rose. She wants Rose to play another part ... she wants her to be the *good* little sister.'

'There isn't any good little sister!' Rose's voice was all high and strangulated. 'There isn't any such part!'

'They're going to write it in,' said Nicola, 'specially for you. Mr Marlowe said you were a proper little trouper, and Mrs French said you'd done a lot of hard work and it wouldn't be fair to – to discard you. So they're going to make this other part, and you're going to come in with the Good Little Boy, and hold his hand, and –'

'I don't want to hold his hand! I don't want another part!' Tears came spurting out of Rose's eyes. 'I want my own part!'

'Hush, now, Rose, there's obviously been some mistake. Did you tell Mrs French, as I told you –' her mother looked at Nicola, mistrustfully, '– that the reason Rose couldn't come to rehearsal this evening was because you'd made her sniff powder up her nose?'

Nicola nodded.

'*Did* you?'

'Yes! I did! That's why she made me take her

place. She said I'd got to pay pence.'

'Pay pence?' Mrs Bruce looked bewildered. 'What are you talking about?'

'What she said … she said I'd got to pay pence.'

'Penance,' said Mr Bruce. 'Do I take it we have some sort of crisis on our hands?'

Mrs Bruce tightened her lips.

'Nothing we can't get sorted out. Rose, do for heaven's sake stop making that noise! How can I get to the bottom of things if I can't hear myself speak?'

Rose subsided, snuffling, into her dressing gown. Mr Bruce, shaking his head, disappeared into his paper. He usually washed his hands of it when it came to what he called 'female squabbles'.

'Now, then!' Mrs Bruce turned back again to Nicola. Her voice was brisk and businesslike. It was the voice she used when she suspected someone of not telling her the entire truth. It meant, *let us get down to brass tacks and have no more of this nonsense.* 'What exactly did Mrs French say?'

'She said, how would I feel like playing the part of the Bad Little Girl all the time.'

'Instead of Rose?'

'It's because of the mouse. Rose can't do the mouse the same as I can.'

'Yes, I can!' Rose sat bolt upright on the sofa.

'No, you can't,' said Nicola. 'You don't like mice.'

'What's that matter? It's not a *real* mouse.'

'But you have to pretend that it is! You have to *feel* it –'

'I do feel it! I feel it all wriggling and horrible!'

'If you thought it was horrible,' said Nicola, 'you wouldn't have it with you in the first place.'

'Yes, I would!'

'No, you –'

'Do they have to?' said Mr Bruce.

'No, they don't.' Mrs Bruce spoke scoldingly. 'Be quiet, the pair of you! This is ridiculous. How can Nicola possibly take over the part at this late stage? Rose has been rehearsing it for weeks.'

'Anyway, what's *she* know about it?' Rose jerked her head, pettishly, in Nicola's direction. '*She's* never acted.'

'Quite. I really think, Nicola, you're being just a tiny bit selfish. When it's Rose who's done all the hard preliminary work – just to come waltzing in and reap the benefit. It's not very sisterly, is it?'

Nicola stuck out her lower lip. Her mother, seeing it, changed tack. Her voice became coaxing.

'You know how much it means to Rose. For you, it's just fun. For Rose – well! For Rose it's everything. After all, she's the one who's going to make it her career. It really means something to Rose. Surely –'

She broke off and smiled, hopefully. Nicola said nothing. She could be stubborn, when she wanted; and now that she'd got the part, she certainly wasn't going to be talked into giving it up just to satisfy Rose.

'Make her!' Rose's voice rang out, shrill and accusing from the sofa. 'Make her say she won't do it!'

'I can't make her,' said Mrs Bruce. 'It must be Nicola's own decision.'

Her father lowered his paper and looked at Nicola over the top of it.

'I suppose you couldn't just say yes and keep them happy?'

Why should I? thought Nicola.

'After all … anything for a quiet life.' Mr Bruce winked at her. He quite often winked at Nicola over the heads of Rose and her mother. It was supposed to convey a sense of fellow feeling: Us Lads against Them Womenfolk. Usually she responded, but today she did not. She just went on standing there, stony-faced, in silence.

'No?' said Mr Bruce. 'In that case –' he raised his paper again, '– there's nothing more to be said. She's been offered the part, she obviously wants to do it, so let's not have any argument. Rose will just have to take a back seat for once.'

Mrs Bruce looked at her husband, frowningly.

'It really isn't playing fair, to take away a part that's already been given to someone else … I'm surprised that Mrs French would do such a thing.'

'But I was the one she wanted all along!'

The words had slipped out before she could stop them. Mrs Bruce turned, sharply.

'How do you know?'

'Because – because she told me.'

'She didn't,' screamed Rose. 'It's a lie!'

''Tisn't a lie!'

44

'It is! It is! Why should anyone want you? You can't dance! You can't –'

'Rose, be quiet! *And* you, Nicola. Brawling like a couple of alley cats. You can both get up to bed.'

It was rare for Mrs Bruce to grow as cross with Rose as she did with Nicola. Rose pouted, but none the less humped herself off the sofa. She trailed rebelliously in Nicola's wake to the door.

'Good,' said Mr Bruce. He rustled his newspaper. 'If that's all settled –'

'It's not all settled.' Mrs Bruce plumped up the cushion where Rose had been sitting. 'As soon as you two get back from school tomorrow we're going down the road to talk to Mrs French. We'll see what *she* has to say about it. In the meantime, you can both of you get upstairs and put yourselves to bed … I've had quite enough of your bickering for one evening!'

The next day, after tea, both Rose and Nicola were marched down the road to Mrs French. They stood on the front steps behind their mother as she knocked at the door with the lion's head knocker.

'Now you'll see,' said Rose.

They were the first words she had addressed to Nicola all day. Nicola didn't deign to reply. She was thinking, If Mrs French lets her have the part back, it will be the meanest thing I ever heard …

It was Mr French who opened the door – at least, Nicola assumed that it was Mr French. He was youngish, and good-looking, with long, curly black hair and a gold chain round his neck with a medallion hanging from it. When Mrs Bruce explained that they had come to see Mrs French, he twisted round to look at a grandfather clock in the hall and said, 'Can you bear to wait five minutes? She won't be long, she's just giving a class. Due to finish any time now.'

He led them through into a front room, which was cluttered with books and stacks of gramophone records.

'Sorry about the mess – we've never quite got around to finding a home for everything. We're still having the place done up, which means only half the rooms are habitable. Now, what can I offer you? Can I offer you coffee? No? You're sure? Well, in that case perhaps you'll excuse me if I slope off. She shouldn't be too long.'

As Mr French left the room, Rose turned excitedly to her mother.

'I didn't know Mrs French gave *classes*.'

'I expect they need the money. Big place like this … must cost a lot to keep up.'

Rose clearly wasn't interested in what things cost to keep up: her mind was running on quite other lines.

'Do you think *I* could have classes with her?'

'You?' Mrs Bruce looked at her in surprise. 'Why should you want classes with her? What's wrong with Madam Paula?'

'Nothing,' said Rose. 'But Mrs *French* used to be with the Royal Ballet.'

'That doesn't necessarily make her a good

teacher. In any case, you don't want to specialize in ballet. You've always said you want to be in musicals.'

'She's changed her mind,' said Nicola. 'She wants to go to the Royal Ballet School now.'

'*Do* you?'

Rose had turned pink beneath her freckles. She shot Nicola a venomous glare.

'I've always wanted to.'

'I never knew that! Why on earth didn't you say so before?'

''Cos she never thought of it before.'

'Yes, I did! I thought of it –'

'Enough!' Mrs Bruce held up a hand. 'Don't for heaven's sake start that again.'

'But I did think of it before! I thought of it *ages* ago.'

'Then you should have said ages ago. We could have done something about it.'

'We still could,' said Rose. 'You don't start there till you're eleven. If I could have classes with Mrs French – *can* I have classes with Mrs French?'

'But what about Madam Paula? She mightn't like it.'

'It wouldn't matter about Madam Paula if I was going to the Royal Ballet School … *can* I? *Please?* Say that I can!'

'Well … I don't know. I suppose, if you're really set on it –'

'I *am*,' said Rose. '*Honestly*. I really *am*. I've been set on it for *years*. I've –'

'All right, all right! You've made your point. I believe you.'

'So will you ask her? This evening? *Will* you?'

'Yes, yes. I'll ask her this evening … as your father would say, anything for a quiet life.'

Rose beamed, triumphantly, in Nicola's direction: she'd got her own way again. She was *always* getting her own way.

Mrs French came in wearing black tights and a sweater, with her hair pulled back into a knot, the way it had been that first day, on the building site.

'Hello, Mrs Bruce! Rose, Nicola … what's all this?' She laughed. 'A deputation?'

Nicola, embarrassed, sat on her hands on the extreme edge of an armchair, whilst Rose moved up closer to her mother on the sofa.

'I hope it's not inconveniencing you.'

Mrs Bruce made it sound as though even if it were she had no intention of going away again. Nicola cringed. If the armchair had had a cushion she would have put it on her head and pretended not to be there. As it hadn't, she kept her eyes fixed firmly on a pile of books, which had been stacked in the hearth. The top one was called *Theatre Street* by somebody whose name she couldn't pronounce: Tamara Kar-sav-in-a. She heard Mrs French say, 'No, not at all! As a matter of fact, I'd just come to the end of a class, so you chose a good moment – that's a very famous book, by the way, Nicola. Written by a famous Russian ballerina. You can borrow it, if you like.'

'Can I?' Nicola looked up, avidly. She liked it

when people offered to lend you their books: it showed they trusted you.

'Remind me to let you have it before you leave.' Mrs French perched herself amiably on the arm of another chair, similar to the one that Nicola was sitting in. 'You might like to read it as well, Rose. It's all about life in a Russian ballet school.'

Rose looked dubious: she wasn't much of a reader. She tugged, impatiently, at her mother's arm. Mrs Bruce, who had been starting to say something, broke off.

'What?' She bent her head. Rose whispered, urgently. 'Oh, yes! All right. Let's get that out of the way first ... Rose is nagging me to know whether it would be possible for her to take some classes with you. Apparently, she's set her heart on going to the Royal Ballet School –'

'The Royal *Ballet* School?'

The way Mrs French said it, Nicola was pleased to note, she made it sound as if Rose were asking to have tea with the Queen. She couldn't have made it clearer that in her opinion Rose didn't stand a chance. A warm glow of satisfaction slowly spread itself through Nicola's body. So much for Rose. Maybe she *wasn't* so wonderful, after all.

'It's an extremely difficult place to get into, you know.'

'I know,' said Rose. She sounded complacent: if anyone could get in there, *she* should be able to.

'Did you know that out of every four hundred applicants only about thirty are chosen? And at least ten of those will be boys?'

Rose made a little pouting motion with her lips.

'She has been dancing a long time,' said Mrs Bruce. 'Ever since she was four years old. She's had a lot of experience.'

'Ah, but it's not just a question of experience, Mrs Bruce –'

'You need gold medals.' Nicola couldn't help it: she *had* to say it. 'You need gold medals, don't you?'

'Well, no, as a matter of fact, you don't! You not only don't need gold medals, you don't even need to have done a step of ballet in your life. In fact, sometimes they prefer it if people haven't because it means they won't have been able to develop any bad habits.'

'I'm sure Rose hasn't developed any bad habits,' said Mrs Bruce.

'Well, no, it's quite possible that she hasn't. I'm just pointing out that a totally inexperienced girl stands every bit as much chance of getting in as one who's been doing it since she was a baby … Nicola, for example.' Mrs French paused. 'She'd stand just as much chance as Rose.'

Rose didn't like that. Nicola could see that she didn't. Mrs Bruce, quite plainly, didn't believe it.

'Surely,' she said, 'there has to be natural talent?'

'Oh, yes! Yes, that's the very thing they're looking for – that plus the right physique. Lots of girls are turned down simply because they don't meet the physical requirements. It doesn't mean they can't still go on to be dancers. There's no reason on earth why Rose shouldn't have a go, if she wants. I'm just warning her not to be disappointed, that's all.'

'Perhaps if she were to take a few classes with you first –'

'I'm afraid that wouldn't be possible, Mrs Bruce. You see, I don't teach full time – I only take a very few selected pupils. Usually girls who are already in the profession. I very very rarely work with the younger ones. Only in the most exceptional cases.'

Mrs Bruce bristled slightly: she was accustomed to think of Rose as being exceptional.

'You know what I feel?' said Mrs French. 'I feel that Rose is far too much of an all-round performer to tie herself down to just one branch of show business. Especially ballet, which is so restricting. Where does she have classes at the moment?'

'She goes to Madam Paula's. It's where she's always gone.'

'Then I think that's exactly where she ought to keep on going. It'll not only give her a good general grounding as a dancer, it'll provide her with the opportunity to develop any other talents she may have, as well. Who knows? She might have potential as an actress, or a singer –'

'Oh, she has.' Mrs Bruce nodded. 'Madam Paula's already told us. In fact, she's going up to London for an audition later this month. It's for *Little Women – The March Girls*, they're calling it. We're hoping she might stand a chance as Amy.'

'I'm sure she'd make a lovely Amy.' Mrs French smiled. Rose smiled back, uncertainly. Nicola could tell that she was trying to make up her mind whether the thought of making a lovely Amy was sufficient compensation for not being considered exceptional enough to have classes with Mrs French.

'Even if she doesn't get one of the leads,' said Mrs Bruce, 'I keep telling her, there's bound to be lots of other parts.'

'Well, of course.'

'I always think it's worth trying. It'll stand her in good stead later, when she's doing it for real.'

'Yes, indeed. I'm all for people having a go.'

There was a silence. Nicola looked down again at the pile of books. She didn't know why, but she had the feeling Mrs French wasn't really very interested in Rose. It was odd, because people usually were. You'd have thought, being a dancer, that Mrs French would be.

'Anyway –' Mrs Bruce cleared her throat. 'The thing we really came about was this part that Rose is doing for you. Nicola said something about you wanting her to take over. I told her, it's ridiculous, at this late stage. She must have got it wrong.'

'She hasn't got it wrong, Mrs Bruce. I did ask her if she'd like to, but only because we have something else in mind for Rose – we do definitely still want Rose. Did Nicola not tell you?'

'Yes!' Nicola's head jerked up, indignantly. 'I did tell her! I told her you wanted Rose for the youngest sister.'

'That's right,' Mrs French nodded. 'We decided that what we'd like was a Good Little Girl to go with the Good Little Boy – Rose struck us as being the very person. As you say, it is rather late to be changing things round, but Nicola already seemed to know most of the Bad Little Girl's part, and I have every confidence in Rose being able to pick things up just as quickly as if she were a pro – which, indeed, she practically is! Certainly she will be if she gets into the West End.'

Mrs Bruce looked round, doubtfully, at Rose.

'The only thing is, she seems to think it's not a proper part.'

'Oh, but it is! I assure you … we're writing it in specially.'

Rose, burying her head in her mother's shoulder, made some utterance that only Mrs Bruce could hear. Mrs Bruce patted her hand, consolingly.

'I'm sure Mrs French will do what she can. You must remember, though … it's not always the largest parts that are the best parts. Not by any manner of means. Isn't that so?' She appealed to Mrs French, who said, 'Any professional will tell you, Rose … a part's what you make it.'

'Not if it's not a real one.' The words came out, muffled, from Rose's buried head. 'Not if it's just a *pretend* one.'

'But it's not a pretend one! Mrs French has already told you … she's writing it in specially.'

'I don't want it! I want the other one – the one I had before!'

Mrs Bruce looked up; half apologetic, half accusing.

'It is very upsetting for a child, to have something that's been given her suddenly taken away.'

'Yes, I do realize that, Mrs Bruce. That's why I've made sure she's being offered something else.'

'I don't want something else!'

'Not even if it's something that's far better suited to you? Just think! No more horrible mice!'

'She's worked very hard at that mouse,' said Mrs Bruce.

'Yes,' Mrs French sighed. 'We really do appreciate all the work she's put in. That's why we don't want to lose her. But you do know, don't you, Rose –' leaving her perch on the arm of the chair, Mrs French sank down, gracefully, on to her heels beside the still sniffling Rose '– you do know that if you're going to go into the profession you'll have to be prepared to take some pretty hard knocks? It won't do you any good just sitting down and crying – you have to learn to take the rough with the smooth. Things don't always work out just the way we'd like them to. Suppose, for instance, you were offered the part of Amy, and then suddenly the director decided that the girl playing Beth would be better as Amy, and that you'd be better as Beth –'

'I wouldn't mind playing Beth! Beth's a *real* part.'

'But so is the Youngest Sister … I promise you! You'll have plenty of things to do.'

'I don't want to play the Youngest Sister! I want to be the Bad Little Girl!'

Mrs French sat back on her heels. Mrs Bruce looked at her, challengingly, as if to say, 'Well? And what now?' Rose just sat there, weeping. Nicola regarded her sister with contempt. All this fuss over a mere *part*.

'Dear oh dear!' Mrs French shook her head. 'The last thing I wanted to do was cause any unhappiness. I'd hoped I'd managed to find a satisfactory solution ... now what do we do? I can't very well ask Nicola to play the Youngest Sister, can I?'

There was a silence, broken only by Rose's snuffles. Nicola could guess what she was thinking. She was thinking that as far as she was concerned there wasn't any reason why Nicola should be asked to play anything at all. Mrs Bruce was probably thinking exactly the same thing.

'I suppose –' Mrs French spoke pleadingly to Rose '– I suppose you couldn't possibly think of the production as a whole? How much better it would be if we had a really *bad* Bad Little Girl and a really *good* Good Little Sister?'

Rose buttoned her lip.

'No.' Mrs French pulled a rueful face. 'I suppose not. I should have stuck to my guns right at the beginning – it's my own fault. I just didn't want to cause any ructions in the family. Now it looks as though I've caused one anyway.' With an air of somewhat weary resignation, she rose to her feet. 'I honestly don't know what to say, Mrs Bruce. I've offered Rose another part; what more can I do? I can only repeat that we should be extremely sorry to lose her – and that the part *is* a real part, if she cares to make it one. It's entirely up to her. If she's as professional as I think she is ...'

There was a silence, while everybody looked at Rose, and Rose looked at the carpet.

'I'll tell you what.' Mrs French crossed to the door. 'I'll go and make us all a cup of coffee, while Rose sits here and has a think. I'm sure when she's done so she'll realize that things aren't anywhere near as bad as they seem. It's simply a question of changing one part for another. Nothing so very catastrophic.' She held open the door, looking at Nicola as she did so. 'Coming?'

Nicola jumped up, gladly: she was only too pleased to escape. She followed Mrs French down a passage and into a large, Aladdin's cave of a kitchen, with stone flags on the floor and a sink the size of a bath tub, with two of the most enormous taps she had ever seen. In the middle of the flags stood a wooden table about ninety feet long – well, say fifty feet long – at any rate, a great deal longer than the table in Mrs Bruce's kitchen. This table wouldn't even fit *into* Mrs Bruce's kitchen. Mrs French pressed a switch attached to something which looked like a large Thermos flask.

'Tell me –' she began unhooking mugs from a row of hooks on the wall '– does Rose always get whatever she wants?'

'Yes,' said Nicola. 'Usually.'

'What about you? Do you?'

'Well –' She considered the question, trying to be fair. 'Sometimes.'

'Haven't you ever wanted to learn dancing, as Rose does?'

Nicola frowned, and ran a finger along the edge of the table. Once, ages ago – ages and *ages* ago – she had thought that perhaps she might. She had mentioned it one Christmas, when her grandparents had been there. Her grandfather, teasing, had said, 'What! A great lanky beanpole like you?' Her grandmother, trying to be kind, had told her to 'Come on, then! Show us what you can do'; but when she had, they had all laughed at her. Rose had laughed louder than anyone. Mr Bruce, afterwards, feeling sorry for her, had pulled her on to his knee for a cuddle and said, 'She might not be any good at waving her legs in the air, but she makes a smashing centre-forward – don't you, me old Nickers?' She'd given up the idea of dancing classes after that. Dancing was stupid, anyhow. She'd far rather play football.

'No?' Mrs French was looking at her. Nicola hunched a shoulder. 'What made them send Rose for lessons?'

'Don't remember. 'Spect they thought she'd be good at it.'

'And they didn't think you would be?'

'S'pose not.'

'Do *you* think you would be?'

'Don't know.'

'Well, let's have a try,' said Mrs French. She

suddenly left her coffee mugs and advanced upon Nicola round the table. 'How old are you?'

'Eleven,' said Nicola.

'Eleven and how much?'

'Eleven and two months.'

'Right. So let's see what you're like on flexibility … if I support you, how far back can you bend?'

Nicola didn't need support – she could bend as far back as anyone wanted her to. She could go right over and touch the floor. But that wasn't dancing, that was gymnastics. She was quite good at gymnastics. She could turn somersaults and do the splits and walk on her hands, and all sorts of things.

'What about frog's legs?' said Mrs French. 'Stretch out on the – no, wait! It'll be cold. Lie on this –' she snatched a coat off a peg and spread it out. 'Lie on your back, as flat as you can … that's it. Now, put the soles of your feet together and bend your legs outwards as far as they'll go, making sure your knees are touching the floor … that's not bad at all! Quite a lot of natural turn out. What are your feet like?'

'Just feet,' said Nicola, bewildered. Even Rose didn't have special sort of feet. At least, she didn't think she had. She was sure her mother would have mentioned it if she had.

Mrs French laughed.

'Don't look so worried. I'm not looking for extra toes – though if the first three did happen by any chance to be more or less the same length, it would be a distinct advantage. Makes pointe work far easier. Let's have a look. Come on! Up on the table and get

your socks off … mm, well, two the same length.
Good high arches. Any trouble with your ankles?'
  Nicola shook her head. This was all very strange.
She was sure Madam Paula had never made Rose sit

on a table and take her socks off.

The door opened and the curly black head that belonged to Mr French peered round. At the sight of Nicola, bare-footed amongst the coffee mugs, he groaned and said, 'Why is it one can never get away from feet in this house?'

'Because feet are important.' Mrs French handed Nicola her socks back. 'I'm glad to say that Nicola's passed the test with flying colours.'

'Bully for Nicola … can I scrounge a coffee?'

'Oh, God, I forgot about it!' Mrs French flew back across the room to the Thermos flask. 'Nicola, I didn't ask you … do you drink coffee, or would you rather have milk?'

'Rose has milk,' said Nicola.

'How about you?'

'I don't mind what I have.'

'Spoken bravely,' said Mr French.

They went back to the front room to find Rose still red-faced and tearful but at least no longer weeping.

'I've been telling her,' said Mrs Bruce. 'She's still got her audition to look forward to. She might well get something from that.'

'Indeed she might,' said Mrs French. 'And then think how grand she'd be … we'd have to count ourselves lucky if she even passed the time of day with us!'

Rose puckered her lips, to indicate that she knew very well she was only being humoured. She didn't join in any of the conversation which followed, but

60

kept her head bent over her mug of warm milk, not even looking up when Nicola, rather shyly, asked Mrs French what it had been like to be a soloist with the Royal Ballet. Mrs French shook her head.

'I'm afraid I was only a very minor soloist … I never aspired to the Lilac Fairy or Queen of the Wilis, or anything like that. Peasant pas-de-deux from *Giselle* was about as far as I ever got. I wasn't really the right physical type. My thighs were always too fat, and my knees were too knobbly.'

'I can hardly believe *that*,' protested Mrs Bruce.

'Oh, I promise you, it's quite true … they may not look particularly fat or knobbly just at this moment, but put them under a tutu and you'd soon see what I mean! One really needs legs like Nicola's – nice and long and straight.'

Nicola had never given much thought to her legs. She knew that they were long, because her mother always said she would make a good wading bird, and sometimes she'd heard people describe her as gangling. She hadn't known that they were *nice* and long – or that they were straight. She glanced at them, now, surreptitiously, as they hung down over the edge of the chair. They just looked like ordinary legs to her. Her mother also glanced at them, not quite so surreptitiously.

'Nicola's legs are too thin,' she said. 'Make her look like a crane.'

'Well, it's better than looking like a female hammer thrower … female hammer throwers don't get anywhere; not in ballet. Cranes sometimes do.'

Mrs Bruce didn't say anything to that. There was a pause, then she leaned forward to place her mug back on the tray.

'Come along, you two. It's time we were off.' She took Rose's half-empty mug away from her. 'We've imposed on Mrs French quite long enough.'

'You haven't imposed at all,' said Mrs French. 'I'm glad that you came. I just hope we see both Nicola *and* Rose at our next rehearsal – oh, and by the way, you may be getting a call from our wardrobe mistress some time during the week. She wants to come round and measure up for costumes. I gave her your number. I hope that was all right?'

'Of course. Though whether they'll both – well! We shall have to see. Nicola, if you're taking that book, you make sure you look after it.'

They walked back up the road in silence, Mrs Bruce in the lead, Nicola, clutching her book and thinking about her legs (nice and long ... *and* straight) a few paces behind, and Rose, who usually skipped and hopped and danced about, morosely dragging her feet in the rear. As they reached the house, Mrs Bruce, holding the gate, said, 'Well?' It seemed to be directed at Nicola. It couldn't really be directed at anyone else – Rose was still trailing, several yards behind. Nicola looked at her mother, warily.

'What?'

'You're determined not to let Rose have her part back again?'

'It's not her part.' Jealously, she hugged *Theatre*

Street to her chest. Mrs French had lent it to *her*, just as she'd given the part of the Bad Little Girl to her. 'It's my part.'

'It *was* Rose's before.'

No, it wasn't, thought Nicola. It was always mine. She walked through the gate.

'She can do the other one – the one they're writing in for her.'

'I won't!' Rose's voice came shrilly from somewhere outside in the road. 'If I can't do the part I want, I won't do any!'

Under cover of the darkness, Nicola pulled one of her squint-eyed faces and stuck out her tongue; then she turned, and stumped off up the path. If Rose wanted to cut herself out entirely, then that was her problem.

The King and Us

by Jhanna N. Malcolm

'Wow, this is a zoo!' Gwen said as the girls filed into the backstage lounge of the Carousel Dinner Theatre on Monday.

Children of all ages sprawled on the tiled floor, chattering noisily. Meanwhile their mothers had taken up all of the available seats in the cramped room. Four of them sat side by side on an old grey Naugahyde couch in the corner, while three others shared an armchair by the door, one on the cushion with the other two perched on the arms. Another woman wearing a lot of make-up had settled herself among the old magazines littering a rickety coffee table. Everyone was busily filling out audition forms.

'All of Deerfield must have turned out for this thing,' Rocky groaned.

'You don't see the Bunheads, do you?' McGee stood on tiptoe and peered over to where several people had gathered along a counter that held a coffee pot and several Styrofoam cups.

Zan, who was the tallest of the gang, shook her head. She could hardly talk. It hadn't occurred to her until this moment that *other* people might attend the auditions, or even worse, they might be *watching* them audition. Her stage fright reappeared with a vengeance. 'Are we sure we want to do this?' Zan whispered hoarsely. 'I mean, it looks like they've already got all the kids they'll need.'

'Of course we want to do this,' Mary Bubnik replied, giving Zan a little shove to prod her into the room. 'We want to meet Nicholas Blade, don't we?'

At the mention of the TV star, Zan felt goose-bumps prickle up and down her arm. She took a deep breath and reminded herself that, after all, Nicholas Blade *was* her hero. She couldn't let a little case of nerves get in the way of meeting him.

'May I have your attention, please?' A chunky girl with cropped blonde hair stood in the doorway behind the gang. She wore a plaid shirt with tan trousers. A dozen keys clinked from a chain hanging from her belt. 'I'm Melissa Davidson, the stage manager, and I'll be running the auditions this after-noon. You can call me Mel.' She held up a clipboard for everyone to see. 'This is the sign-in sheet. I'll leave it here in the green room by the coffee machine.'

'This room's not green,' Mary Bubnik observed loudly.

Mel heard her and chuckled. 'I know it's not. But it's a theatre tradition to call the lounge the "green room". Don't ask me why.' She shrugged. 'Maybe because this is where actors used to get paid after their performances.'

'Then they should paint it green so people don't get confused,' Mary Bubnik whispered to Rocky, who motioned her to be silent.

'Please print your name clearly on this list,' Mel continued. 'And then we can begin auditions.'

Several of the mothers clutched their children by the hand and rushed forward.

'Jason needs to go first,' one of them cried, lifting a startled-looking boy up over the head of the girl in front of him and dropping him at the stage manager's feet.

'Oh, no, you don't!' a large woman in a flowered print dress shouted, shoving her daughter ahead of Jason.

The woman with all the make-up checked her watch and declared, 'I absolutely have to leave in half an hour. My daughter must go *now*.'

'You should have thought of that before you arrived,' another woman shot back. 'Timothy and I were here first, and we'll be going first.'

The women began to argue shrilly as the stage manager tried to restore order.

'Those are what's known as "stage mothers",' Rocky whispered out of the corner of her mouth. 'They couldn't be in a play when they were little, so they force their kids to be in them now.'

'They're not going to be in the show, are they?' Mary Bubnik asked, imagining how unpleasant that would be.

Rocky waved one hand. 'Naw. They'll just hang around before and after rehearsals, getting in everybody's way, until opening night, when the stage manager will make them go and sit in the audience where they belong.'

A shrill blast from a police whistle brought all the clamour to a standstill. Mel took the whistle from her mouth and smiled pleasantly. 'Thank you. As I said, we'll see each child in the order they sign in. No exceptions.'

She set the clipboard on the counter and quickly left the room. There was a mad dash as each of the mothers tried to be first to get on the list. McGee and the others worked their way through the crowd and finally were able to write down their names. Then the stage manager brought in some folding chairs, and the gang scrambled to sit in them.

'You girls get audition forms?' Mel asked.

They shook their heads. 'We just got here,' Gwen explained.

The stage manager handed each of them a form. 'Write your name and a phone number where you can be reached at the top. Then list your experience and any conflicts you might have.'

A mother sitting on the couch beside a tiny girl with glasses raised her hand. 'What kind of experience do you mean?'

Mel ran her hand through her hair. 'Any plays or performances the kids might have been in. What kind of dance or voice lessons they've taken – that sort of thing.'

'We can put down *The Nutcracker*,' Mary Bubnik whispered. 'That should impress them.'

'Also that we study at the Deerfield Academy of Dance,' Zan added. 'The best ballet school in Ohio.'

As she headed for the door that led to the stage, Mel called over her shoulder, 'The director will talk with all of you in just a minute, then we'll begin.'

Several teenaged girls sat cross-legged on the floor, using each other's backs as tables to fill out their forms.

'Oh, darn,' a pretty blonde with waist-length hair exclaimed, 'there's not enough room to list all the plays I've done. I mean, I put down *Alice in Wonderland* and that took up almost the entire line.'

The girl whose back she was using said, 'Flip the paper over. I was able to list all the plays we did at the Deerfield Children's Theatre, plus my work with the puppet group, Hand Jive.'

This time it was Mary who murmured, 'Gee, maybe Zan's right. Maybe they do have enough experienced people already.'

'They're just trying to psych us out,' Rocky replied. 'Besides, the notice said the director needed kids. Those girls look at least eighteen. I bet they're too old.'

Gwen was the first to finish filling out her form. Under 'Experience' she had listed *The Nutcracker*, and all her years of piano lessons. For a moment she'd considered mentioning the part she'd played in her science class play at school. But she was afraid the director would ask what it was and then she'd have to tell him she'd been a toad eating flies to demonstrate the food chain. That would be too embarrassing.

Gwen stood up and handed her audition sheet to Mel. Then she spotted several people coming through the stage door and bolted back to her seat with her friends. 'Don't look now,' she hissed, 'but directly behind you is the cutest guy in the whole wide world!'

'Where?' Mary Bubnik started to turn around when Gwen punched her on the shoulder.

'I said, *don't look*,' Gwen hissed. 'He's standing in the doorway with two other boys.'

'Don't worry,' Mary said, 'I'll be subtle.' She grabbed her small pink purse and made a big show of dropping it on the floor. Then she bent down to pick it up, twisting backwards to get a good look at the door. In the process she leaned over too far and her folding chair tipped over, hitting the floor with a loud boom. As she fell, Mary reached out and grabbed Zan by the arm, pulling her down with her.

'Yeow!' Zan shrieked, more in surprise than hurt.

Gwen rolled her eyes at the ceiling. 'Very subtle.'

McGee rushed over to see if Zan and Mary Bubnik were all right. They were sitting on the floor, giggling like maniacs.

'I can't believe they're doing that,' Rocky whispered to Gwen. 'They're going to make us all look like a bunch of geeks.' Rocky flipped up the collar of her jacket and she and Gwen both slumped down in their folding chairs trying to hide their faces.

As McGee pulled a hysterical Mary to her feet, she looked directly into the cute boy's dark brown eyes. Without thinking, she smiled at him. To her delight he smiled back, and McGee thought she would melt right into the ground.

She completely forgot about Zan, who was sitting on the floor with her hand outstretched, and hurried back to her seat next to Rocky. McGee quickly removed her baseball cap and tried to smooth out the tufts of hair that had come out of her braids. She made a secret vow to herself that, if he talked to her, she wouldn't even mention sports.

'Oh, no!' Rocky whispered. 'He's coming this way.'

'Don't move!' Gwen gasped.

The boy stepped in front of the girls, put his name on the sign-in sheet, and then stopped in front of McGee. 'Aren't you on Fairview's baseball team?' he asked.

Up until that instant McGee had been very proud of her team, and especially of the fact that she was their star catcher. Now she wished she'd never heard of them. McGee bit her lip uncertainly. If she said yes, this cute boy would think she was just another jock, and that would be that.

She hesitated for a second. Finally McGee shook her head. 'No. I'm not.'

'Oh, gee, I'm sorry.' His warm brown eyes were filled with disappointment. 'You look just like this girl that plays for them.' Then he smiled and added, 'She's really terrific.'

'Oh, thank –' McGee swallowed hard. How could she thank him? She had to keep pretending it wasn't her. Instead she said, 'Do you like sports?'

'Yeah, but I never get to do them much any more.' He gestured toward the stage and added, 'Since I've started working here.'

Mel reappeared at the stage door. 'Say, Brett, the director wants to talk to you for a minute.'

The boy named Brett waved in acknowledgement, then turned back to McGee. 'Got to go. See you later.'

McGee nodded silently. She didn't trust her voice to speak.

'He must be in the play,' Gwen said.

'He is,' one of the girls sitting across from them declared. 'He plays the King's oldest son.'

'I wonder how he got that part?' Mary Bubnik wondered out loud. 'The auditions haven't even started.'

'That's Brett Allen,' the blonde said. 'He's done tons of shows here. He started in *The Music Man*, and then last year he was one of the leads in *A Thousand Clowns*.'

Her friend sighed. 'I saw it twice. Brett was great.'

Zan, who had managed to pick herself up and sit back in her chair, said, 'I think he's cute, but I'm saving myself for Nicholas Blade.'

'Me, too,' Mary Bubnik agreed. 'Now *that's* good-looking.'

'All right, listen up, everyone,' Mel shouted. 'The director wants everyone to come into the theatre. Follow me.' There was a nervous scuffling of chairs and papers as everyone jumped up and left the room behind her.

McGee and the gang followed the crowd out into the auditorium. A tall, thin man in jeans and a purple polo shirt was leaning against the stage. A white sweater was looped around his neck, and a pair of sunglasses rested on top of his salt-and-pepper hair. Another pair of reading glasses rested on the top of his nose. He carried stacks of pictures and a worn yellow copy of the script for *The King and I*.

'Good afternoon, everyone,' he announced in a deep voice that echoed around the theatre. 'I'm Hayden Wilson, the director of this little masterpiece.'

A couple of his assistants, who were lounging in the front row seats, chuckled loudly.

'Now, we want to move these auditions along as smoothly as possible,' the director continued. 'You'll each get your turn, but when Mel, my better half here, says you are through – please, leave the stage.' He gestured toward a chubby fellow sitting at an upright piano in the aisle. 'Johnny Ogden, our faithful accompanist, will play your sheet music, if you have any. I only want to hear a few bars of a song.'

Johnny Ogden, whose red hair looked like someone had stuck a Brillo pad on top of his head, waved pleasantly.

'Basically, what we're looking for today are fifteen Asian children to play our King's kids,' Hayden Wilson declared.

There was a loud murmur as the parents and children looked nervously over their shoulders and at the hopefuls milling around them.

'Looks like she's a shoo-in,' Rocky whispered, pointing to a tiny Japanese girl who clung to her mother by one of the exits.

The director chuckled loudly. 'Obviously, many of you will have to wear make-up to look Asian. But Monty and Cheryl' – he pointed to a boy and girl wearing white smocks – 'are our wizards of disguise, and will take care of all that.'

The teenaged girls who'd been sitting on the floor talking about their theatre experiences burst into applause. One of them even shouted, 'Way to go, Monty and Cheryl!'

'What is this?' Gwen murmured. 'A private club? It looks like everyone already knows each other.'

'I know.' Mary Bubnik nodded, a worried frown creasing her forehead. 'We're never going to get in this play.'

'Everyone has an equal chance to be cast,' Mr Wilson announced. 'Now I'm looking for energy, energy, *energy*.' He pounded his fist in his palm dramatically as he repeated the word. 'That's why I've had everyone come into the theatre to watch. We'll be your audience, so I want each of you to give it your best shot.'

McGee's eyes turned to huge saucers in her face. 'Brett, too?' she whispered to Rocky.

Rocky shrugged. 'It looks like it.'

McGee shook her head so hard her braids swung across her face. 'I can't do it.'

'Me, neither,' Zan gasped, her knees suddenly feeling a little wobbly.

Hayden Wilson gestured to the stage manager, who handed him the piece of paper Gwen had handed her. He glanced at it briefly, then declared, 'All right, it looks like Gwendolyn Hays will be first.'

'First!' Gwen squeaked. 'I – I can't.'

The director peered over the top of his half glasses. 'What do you mean, you can't?' His voice was ominously low and calm. 'If you can't, then what in heaven's name are you doing here?'

Everyone turned to stare at Gwen. She felt her cheeks grow hot with embarrassment and knew she must look like a bright cherry with freckles. 'I mean, I can't do it *alone*.' She turned, looking meaningfully at her friends. 'Our song is a *group* song.'

The director fluttered his hand impatiently. 'Whatever. Let's just keep this thing moving.'

Zan and McGee had decided to beat a hasty retreat and were headed for the door. But Rocky grabbed each of them firmly by the hand and dragged them up the steps on to the stage. The lights had been turned on and they stood blinking out into the darkness of the auditorium.

'All right, group,' the director said sarcastically, 'what are you going to do for us today?'

None of them could speak. They hadn't had a chance to discuss their song. Finally Mary Bubnik stepped forward and announced brightly, 'We'll be doing "I'm a Little Teapot".' She paused, then added, 'With all of the movements.'

A loud groan sounded from the gang.

'Mark my words, Mary Bubnik,' Rocky muttered

under her breath, 'if we live through this, I'm going to kill you!'

'Hays Mortuary – you stab 'em, we slab 'em!' Gwen cradled the phone receiver against her ear as she dug into the cookie jar on the kitchen counter. It was Wednesday after school, and the phone had been ringing when she walked into the house. She stuffed a huge oatmeal cookie into her mouth and waited for the caller to respond.

There was a long silence on the other end.

'Hello?' Gwen mumbled with a full mouth. 'Anybody there?'

Finally a female voice said brusquely, 'I'm trying to reach Gwendolyn Hays. Have I dialled the right number?'

The voice sounded like old lady Phelps, the grumpy secretary at Gwen's school, whom nobody liked. Gwen reached for another cookie and took a loud crunchy bite. 'Who wants to know?'

'The Carousel Dinner Theatre.'

Gwen's eyes widened, and she nearly choked on her cookie crumbs. After the gang's audition on Monday she'd been convinced they'd never hear from the theatre again. She still got embarrassed thinking about standing on the stage in front of the director, his assistants, and that cute boy, Brett, pretending to be a teapot. It wouldn't have been so bad if Mary hadn't been so off-key. And now some official from the theatre wanted to speak to her, and she'd just acted like a total jerk.

'Uh, just a minute,' Gwen said, pretending to be her own sister. 'I'll see if Gwen's home yet from her, uh, piano lesson.' She put her hand over the phone and shouted loudly, 'Gwen, it's for you.'

She held the receiver at arm's length and

called in a thin, high-pitched cry, as if the voice were coming from the other side of the house, 'I'm co-o-o-m m-ming!'

Then Gwen pointed the receiver down at her feet and ran in place softly, gradually making her footsteps louder to make it sound like she was running to the phone. While she ran Gwen struggled to swallow the rest of her cookie and cleared her throat.

Finally she put the phone up to her mouth, and lowering her voice to what she hoped was a mature tone, said, 'This is Gwendolyn Hays.'

'Gwen? This is Melissa Davidson, the stage manager from the Carousel Dinner Theatre.'

'Oh, *hello!*' Gwen affected a surprised tone. Then she added, 'I have to apologize for my little sister, who answered the phone. She's not always dealing with a full deck.'

Mel chuckled. 'That's all right. I just wanted to let you know that you've been cast in *The King and I*.'

'I have?' Gwen squealed, forgetting all about disguising her voice. 'That's great!'

'The first rehearsal for you will be this Thursday evening at seven p.m.'

'Will Nicholas Blade be there?'

'I'm sure he will,' Mel replied. 'He's already been rehearsing for two weeks.'

'Great!' Gwen closed her eyes and imagined the handsome star sitting in one of those canvas chairs with his name printed on the back, a pair of sunglasses perched on top of his head.

'Now, remember,' Mel continued, 'Thursday, downstairs at the theatre. Be on time, and wear comfortable clothes. 'Bye now.'

'Wait!' Gwen yelled into the phone but it was too late. All she heard was a dial tone. The stage manager hung up before she'd had a chance to ask her if the rest of the gang had made it into the play.

Gwen hung up the phone and turned to see her older brother Danny leaning against the doorframe, with his arms crossed and a superior smile on his face. He was tall and skinny as a rake, with black, slicked-back hair and square, dark-framed glasses. Danny spent most of his time at the library and looked just like what he was, the senior class brain.

'How long have you been standing there?' Gwen demanded.

'Long enough to witness your entire performance.' Danny shook his head. He imitated her pretending to call herself and running in place by the phone. 'That was the dumbest thing I've ever seen.'

Normally her brother's needling got to her, but not today. Gwen looked him straight in the eye and said airily, 'That performance, plus my superior musical talents, has just won me a part at the Carousel Dinner Theatre.' She added casually, 'I'll be co-starring with Nicholas Blade.'

'Nicholas Blade?' Her brother dropped his arms to his side, a startled look on his face.

'That's right,' Gwen replied, reaching for another cookie. 'You remember him, don't you? The famous TV star?'

Danny squinted at her suspiciously. 'You're kidding.' Then he added, less confidently, 'Aren't you?'

Gwen shrugged nonchalantly. 'Show up on opening night, and we'll see who's kidding.'

From the dazzled look on her brother's face, she could tell that he was not just impressed, but *very* impressed. This was Gwen's moment of triumph and she knew it. 'Maybe, if you're nice, I can get an autograph for you.'

Before he could say a word, Gwen swept grandly through the living room and into her bedroom. As soon as she had shut the door behind her, and she knew no one could see her, Gwen jumped up and down in a circle, hugging herself and squealing, 'I got it! I got it!'

Just as quickly, she stopped. 'What if I'm the only one of us in the play?' Gwen murmured out loud. 'I'll have to be singing and dancing with complete strangers on a stage in front of hundreds of people.' She shuddered at the thought. 'That would be awful!' Gwen snatched up the pink Princess phone and quickly dialled a number.

'Reed residence, Zan speaking,' a familiar soft voice answered.

Gwen got right to the point. 'Zan, it's Gwen. I'm in the play. Are you?'

'*Yes!*' Zan shouted in her ear. 'Mel just called to tell me. Isn't it truly wonderful?'

'Fantastic!' Gwen bellowed, not caring whether her brother heard her enthusiasm. 'I was afraid I'd have to go it alone.'

'I'm so glad you called. I was too nervous to phone you. I wonder if the rest of the gang made it in?'

'Hang up!' Gwen ordered. 'And let's call them. You take Rocky, and I'll call McGee and Mary Bubnik.'

The girls slammed down their phones without even saying goodbye. Zan flopped across the green-and-white quilt covering her brass bed and punched in Rocky's number. Although the rest of her parents' house was ultra modern, Zan had insisted on having an old-fashioned bedroom. Little white lace pillows were neatly arranged along the headboard. She hugged one to her chest as she listened to the phone ring.

'Yeah?'

It was one of Rocky's brothers. Zan could hear the television playing at full volume in the background. 'May I speak to Rocky, please?' she asked politely.

'Yo, Rocky. It's for you.' Rocky's brother yelled so loudly that Zan had to hold the phone away from her ear.

'Who is it?' Zan heard Rocky shout back in the distance.

'Your friend,' he bellowed.

'Which one?'

'I didn't know you had more than one,' her brother retorted.

'Ask who it is, Michael,' Rocky shouted.

'Look, I'm not your secretary.' There was a loud clunking sound as Michael dropped the phone to the floor. Zan heard pounding footsteps as Rocky's voice shouted, 'What did you do that for, you jerk?'

'My arm was getting tired,' Michael drawled.

Before Rocky could get into a shouting match with her brother, Zan yelled, 'Rocky, it's Zan. Pick up the phone.'

'Zan? Sorry about Michael. He's a total slime, but I was trying to watch *Nicholas Blade, Private Eye*.'

'Is it on now?' Zan said, checking the slim gold watch on her wrist.

'Yeah, they just rolled the opening titles. Now they're showing some dumb deodorant commercial so we have a minute to talk.'

'I just wanted to see if you got cast in *The King and I*.'

'Sure,' Rocky replied. 'And so did everybody else.'

'Even Mary Bubnik?'

'Yeah. I guess not being able to sing on-key or walk straight didn't matter.'

'How did you find out?'

'I asked. Hey, Nick's back on. Catch you later.'

Zan winced as Rocky banged her phone down on its hook. She stared at the receiver and shook her head. 'Doesn't anyone say goodbye any more?'

Gwen called McGee and the two girls didn't say a word, they just squealed for a full minute. Then Gwen said, 'I have to call Mary Bubnik. I'll talk to you later.'

When Mary Bubnik heard the good news she shouted, 'I just can't believe it! Me and Nicholas Blade together on the same stage, in the same theatre, singing the same songs –'

'Hopefully in the same key,' Gwen murmured under her breath.

Mary didn't hear her remark but continued, 'My mom is so excited, she's already talking about buying me some new outfits.'

Gwen stuck her hand in the cookie jar, then stopped. 'I'm starting a whole new diet just for Nicholas,' she announced dramatically. 'I'm cutting out Twinkies completely.'

Mary was suitably impressed. Twinkies were Gwen's favourite food. The two girls talked about what they would wear to the first rehearsal, and what they would say to Nicholas Blade when they first met him.

Suddenly Mary Bubnik giggled. 'I just thought of something.'

'What?'

'Now that we're all in the play, it's not *The King and I* any more.'

'What is it, then?'

'The King and *Us*!'

Panic!

by Antonia Barber

'Did you see her face,' asked Jodie gleefully, 'when Mrs Martin said I was doing the solo?'

'She did look a bit fed up,' said Hannah.

'Fed up? She was furious! She was so sure she'd get it.'

It was a warm spring evening and they were walking home from ballet class. There were daffodils in the park and pink blossom on the trees. But all Jodie could see was the angry face of Kelly Johnson.

Hannah sighed: she wished the two would stop quarrelling.

Jodie heard her sigh and said, 'I know it should have been you really. You're the best dancer.'

'No, I'm not,' said Hannah quickly.

'Yes, you are. You got a Distinction in the grade exam and Kelly and me only got Highly Commended.'

Hannah shrugged; she felt quite guilty about that.

'Only you couldn't do it, could you?' Jodie went on. 'You'd be hopeless dancing solo in front of all the parents.'

'Yes,' said Hannah. She wished Jodie would talk about something else.

An only child, Hannah had always been painfully shy. When she was four her mother, worried by a daughter who hid behind chairs when visitors came, decided to take her along to the local dancing class. 'It'll get her used to being with other kids,' she told her friends, 'otherwise I'll have problems when she starts school.' And it had worked because Hannah loved the dancing. 'Took to it like a duck to water,' said her mother proudly. 'The teacher says she's got a gift ... could be a real dancer one day!'

Only I never will be, thought Hannah, because however well I dance, I just can't do it in front of an audience.

About two weeks later, Hannah noticed that Jodie was limping. It was only a very tiny limp and she seemed to be pretending that it wasn't there.

But Sharon, Kelly's best mate, spotted it. 'Hurt your foot, have you, Jodie?' she asked eagerly.

'No!' said Jodie quickly and then, 'Well I sort of sprained it ... but it's better now.'

She watched as Sharon hurried off to report to Kelly. 'They're like vultures,' she told Hannah fiercely, 'waiting for me to drop out so that Kelly can take my place!'

'When did you sprain your ankle?' asked Hannah.

'I didn't,' said Jodie crossly, 'I just said that.'

'So what is it?'

'Well … the thing is … I've got this verruca under my foot … only I don't want *them* to know.'

Hannah could see why. A sprained ankle had a sort of glamour; even a ballerina might get a sprain. But a verruca just made you a joke.

'Will it be better in time for the show?' she asked anxiously.

'I don't know,' said Jodie. 'But if I can't do it, it's not going to be Miss Smarty-Pants Kelly!'

'Who else is there?' said Hannah doubtfully.

'There's you,' said Jodie. 'If I can't do it, you're going to have to dance the solo.'

And when Hannah protested, she added, 'You're my friend, see, and you can't let me down!'

◉

Hannah was dancing before a vast audience of parents … but when she tried to lift her foot it wouldn't move … she felt like a puppet with broken strings … her knees went all over the place and the parents were beginning to laugh at her … She woke suddenly in a cold sweat and realized that it was just another nightmare. I'll never be able to do it, she thought. I don't care what Jodie says. Mrs Martin will know that I can't, I told her before …

What Jodie didn't know was that the ballet teacher had already offered the solo to Hannah, before she gave it to Jodie. She had called at the house to talk to Hannah and her mother.

'I know you're a bit shy,' she said, 'but you did so well in the grade exam, I would like the parents to see how well you dance.'

'Oh, she's always been shy,' said Hannah's mother. 'She used to hide behind chairs when we had visitors.' She laughed cheerfully. Her daughter's shyness seemed to her just a fact of life, as much a part of her as her hair colour or her dark eyes.

Mrs Martin saw it differently. 'Young children are often shy,' she said, 'but with the right help they can grow out of it.'

But Hannah would not be persuaded. She knew she could never do the solo and in any case Jodie had set her heart on it.

But now it was different. Now Jodie wanted her to do it … and she wouldn't take No for an answer.

'We'll get to ballet class early,' she said, 'and ask Mrs Martin if you can do it instead of me. I'm sure she'll let you.'

Hannah knew that Mrs Martin would be delighted and the thought terrified her. But she could see no way out. Jodie was relying on her. If I let her down, thought Hannah, she might not be my best friend any more. She imagined having no one to walk to school with, no one to talk to in the playground … Life would be unbearable.

So she went to class early with Jodie and sure enough Mrs Martin gave her the solo. Kelly wasn't pleased and Hannah felt sorry for her until she heard her arguing with Jodie.

'Hannah's a better dancer than you …' Jodie was saying.

'She's better than you too,' retorted Kelly, 'only

she's got no bottle. Everyone knows that. One look at the audience and she'll be shaking like a jelly!'

'No, she won't!' said Jodie indignantly.

'So you'd better not,' she warned Hannah, 'otherwise Kelly will gloat and I shall look a right idiot!'

Hannah had no problems learning the dance. She practised with Jodie until every step was perfect. When the costumes were ready she began to enjoy it. In a pink tutu decorated with rosebuds, she felt like a real ballerina ... except, of course, that there was no audience. Whenever she thought of the parents, sitting in rows, all staring at her, watching for every little mistake, then her courage failed her. On the night before the concert she couldn't get to sleep. When she did, the nightmare came back and she woke with catcalls and laughter ringing in her ears.

In the changing room, dressing for the performance, she put on the pink tutu and felt like a complete fraud. The others were all chattering cheerfully as they preened in front of the mirror. But Hannah's hands were trembling and she felt suddenly sick.

'Are you OK?' asked one of the kinder girls. 'You look awfully white.'

The pity in her voice was more than Hannah could bear. She rushed into one of the loos and threw up. Leaning against the door while the sick feeling passed, she could hear anxious voices outside. 'She'll never make it ... She always gets in a panic ...' When she came out they stared at her wide-eyed. 'Shall we get Mrs Martin?'

Hannah shook her head. 'Just leave me alone,' she said. 'I'll be better in a minute.'

But no one believed her. She didn't believe it herself.

I have to find Jodie, she thought, and tell her that I can't do it. She'll understand. She'll see I'm not well ...

Jodie was helping Mrs Martin to get the groups of dancers on and off the stage, but when Hannah arrived backstage there was no sign of her. A crowd of younger dancers rushed past, laughing and excited, on their way back to the changing rooms. Everyone else seems to enjoy it, thought Hannah miserably. Why am I the only one who panics?

A group of girls in the wings began to move on to the stage. As their music began Mrs Martin caught sight of Hannah. 'You're next,' she said with a smile and turned away to watch the performance.

Hannah took deep breaths and felt a little calmer. Then Jodie arrived carrying some piano music. 'It was in your car,' she told Mrs Martin and then, turning to Hannah, she said cheerfully, 'You look great!'

Hannah began to think that she might be able to do it after all. Jodie was her best friend and she couldn't let her down. She moved to where she could see beyond the dancers ... to where she could see the audience. It was a big mistake. At the sight of the rows and rows of strange faces, her heart began to race again and her hands started shaking ...

I can't do it, she thought, I was stupid to think that I could … I'll tell Mrs Martin I'm ill.

But just then Jodie turned and caught sight of her friend's white face and her trembling hands. She stared at Hannah for a long moment, frowning. Then her eyes seemed to go as hard as nails. She came close so that Mrs Martin wouldn't hear and hissed, 'You dare to let me down, Hannah, and I will *never ever* speak to you again!'

Hannah stepped back. She felt as if someone had thrown a bucket of cold water in her face. The shock was followed by a rush of anger. How could Jodie speak to her like that? A friend should help when you were in trouble, not *threaten* you! She doesn't care one bit about me, she thought; she's just been using me to get at Kelly. She glared furiously back at Jodie as the music ended and the applause began.

'Ready, Hannah?' asked Mrs Martin as the dancers came running off into the wings.

Hannah took a deep breath and nodded.

The teacher looked at her closely. 'Are you all right?' she asked.

'I'm fine!' said Hannah and suddenly she was. I'll show Jodie, she thought. *I* don't need *her*. And drawing herself up to her full height she ran lightly and confidently on to the stage.

Five minutes later she was back in the wings with the applause of the audience still ringing in her ears.

'Well done, Hannah!' said Mrs Martin smiling at her. 'I knew you could do it.'

'You were brilliant!' said Jodie.

Hannah looked at her coldly and walked away back to the changing room.

The other girls seemed surprised to see her

come back smiling.

'How did it go? Were you all right?' They crowded round.

Hannah could hardly believe that it had gone so well. The audience had felt really friendly and she had actually enjoyed herself once she was on the stage. Maybe I can be a dancer after all, she thought.

Then she remembered Jodie. I didn't let her down, she thought, so I suppose she'll still want to be best friends. But do *I* want *her*? Part of her wanted to pay Jodie back for her meanness … and yet she knew in her heart that she wanted to stay friends.

And then, 'I couldn't think what else to do.'

It was Jodie's voice and Hannah turned to see her friend standing behind her. 'I could tell how scared you were,' Jodie went on, 'and I knew that if I said something kind, you would fall apart.'

Hannah thought for a moment and knew that it was true. 'Yes,' she said honestly, 'I would have done!'

'I thought if I made you even more scared of *not* doing it …' Jodie grinned awkwardly.

Hannah grinned back. 'Actually,' she said, 'it wasn't like that. I just got really mad at you. But it worked anyway.'

'So you see,' said Jodie, 'you couldn't have done it without me.'

'No,' said Hannah, 'I couldn't.' And at once they were friends again.

'You coming back to my house?' asked Jodie.

'I'll have to tell my mum,' said Hannah.

They found her surrounded by other parents all saying how well Hannah had danced. 'I couldn't believe it …' she was telling them, 'I mean, she's always been so shy. When she was little, she used to hide behind chairs …'

'You're going to have to do something about your mum,' said Jodie.

'Yes,' said Hannah, looking very determined. 'She's just told that story for the very last time!'

Boys Don't Do Ballet – Do They?

by Vivian French

'Whoops!' Jenny staggered as she pulled herself round the edge of the kitchen table on pointe. It didn't matter that she was really only balancing on the rubber edges of her school shoes. Inside her head she was pirouetting round and round a darkened stage with one silvery spotlight shining down on her gleaming dark hair ...

'*Jenny!*' Jenny's mum was standing in the kitchen doorway. 'How many times do I have to tell you *not* to do that to your shoes? You'll *ruin* them!'

Jenny gave her mum a guilty grin. 'Sorry,' she said, and hopped into first position.

'Heels together ... feet in a line. Look, Mum! Madam Anna says I have a wonderful turn out!'

'Madam Anna also says that you're still much too young to go on pointe,' Mum said.

Jenny made a face. 'I'm not *much* too young.'

'H'mph.' Mum opened a drawer and slung a handful of knives and forks on the table. 'Here –

dance about and lay for four for supper.'

'Four? Who's coming?' Usually it was only Jenny and her mum.

Mum handed Jenny the salt and pepper. 'Another ballet fan,' she said. 'I was hanging out the washing and I got talking to the new people next door. Mrs Davis told me that her youngest child – Christy, I think she said – really loves ballet. I said you went to Madam Anna's classes, and it ended up with me asking them in for supper.'

'How old is she?' Jenny asked. 'Has she done classes before? She could come with me. I'd look after her – I can show her all the positions. Madam Anna says I'm very good at looking after the little ones. I always tie their ribbons for them.'

'I don't think you'll need to do that for Christy,' Mum said. 'He's a boy.'

Jenny stared at her mum.

'A *boy*? But boys don't do ballet!'

'Of course they do,' Mum said. 'What about Fritz in *The Nutcracker*? And Romeo? And –'

'I didn't mean *that*,' Jenny said. 'I meant, they don't do ballet at Madam Anna's. Well – only the very little boys, and they run about being silly.'

Mum began to laugh. 'Jenny! How do you think male dancers ever got started? They went to classes, just like you!'

Jenny shook her head. 'But I don't *want* boys in our class. They'd spoil it. I know they would.'

Mum was about to say something else when there was a loud *ring!* at the front door.

'There they are! Run and open the door, Jenny.'

'Do I have to?' Jenny asked.

'Yes!' said Mum. 'And hurry up!'

Jenny walked as slowly as she dared to the front door. She could feel Mum hoping that she would be friendly and nice, but she didn't want to be. She and her friends had been going to Madam Anna's for almost as long as she could remember. They had secrets and whispered together and boasted about how Madam Anna said that they were her best class ever. A boy would just get in the way. He wouldn't know what to do. He'd be silly, and rush around shouting, like the little boys. And – Jenny suddenly felt more cheerful – where would he change his clothes? The little boys hopped about in their vests and trunks, but there was nowhere for older boys ... she was almost sure of it. As she opened the door she smiled a sorry-but-it's-no-good smile.

'Hello,' she said to the neat little woman and the boy on the doorstep. 'Do come in. I'm Jenny, but it won't be any good Christy coming to my ballet class because we don't have anywhere for boys to change their clothes.' And she waved them inside.

Mrs Davis looked a little surprised as she walked down the hall into the kitchen. Christy stopped on the doormat. 'It doesn't matter about a place to change,' he said cheerfully to Jenny. 'I always went to class in my tights anyway. I only need to change my shoes. What level are you at? Are you on pointe yet?'

Jenny stared at him. He had a round face with bright red cheeks, and his eyes were very blue. He wasn't exactly fat, but he certainly wasn't thin, and he was only just as tall as she was. He didn't look in the least like any of the pictures of famous dancers she had pinned up in her bedroom. They were thin, and pale, with bony noses and high cheekbones. Christy looked like – Jenny scratched her nose and thought about it. What *did* he look like? Then she realized. Christy looked just like an ordinary boy. And all the ordinary boys Jenny knew liked football, or roller blades, or messing about in the park. They didn't *ever* do ballet.

Christy was staring now, but he was still smiling. 'Don't you speak?' he asked Jenny.

'When I want to,' she said in her most hoity toity voice, and ran into the kitchen where Mrs Davis and Mum were sitting and chatting. Christy came after her, and sat himself down – without waiting to be asked.

'Hi!' he said to Mum, and he beamed his red-cheeked smile. Jenny scowled.

The supper party was not a success. At least, Jenny didn't think so. Mum enjoyed herself, and Mrs Davis talked a great deal, and Christy ate a lot and answered all Mum's questions about school and ballet … but Jenny just wanted them to go away. She put her head right down while she was eating, and afterwards she went to sit at the other end of the room from the others. She didn't want to know that Christy was going to be in her class at school. She didn't want to know that he had won a prize for dancing in a competition. And she *definitely* didn't want to know that Mrs Davis had already spoken to Madam Anna and that Christy was going to come to her class the very next day.

'That's lovely,' said Mum as Mrs Davis and Christy got ready to go. 'Isn't it, Jenny?'

Jenny made a snorting sort of noise.

'Maybe we could share taking and collecting,' said Mrs Davis, and Mum nodded. 'I'd be delighted.'

After Mrs Davis and Christy had gone, Mum began to wash up. 'Jenny,' she said, 'why were you so rude?'

Jenny wriggled. 'I didn't mean to be,' she said.

'Well,' said Mum, 'you were – very. Now, tomorrow Mrs Davis is taking you to ballet, and I want you to be very helpful and look after Christy. Just think how you would feel if you were going to a new class and didn't know anyone.'

Jenny wriggled some more. 'But what will my friends say?'

'It doesn't matter what they say,' Mum said.

Jenny sighed. Obviously Mum didn't understand at all.

Mrs Davis knocked on the door the next day at a quarter to four. For the first time in her life Jenny wasn't looking forward to ballet class, and she wasn't ready. Mum scooped up her leotard and pink tights and pushed them into her bag.

'Come on, Jenny,' she said, and she walked with Jenny to Mrs Davis's car. Christy was already sitting in the back, wearing a stripy jumper and baggy green trousers. Jenny sniffed as she got in beside him.

99

'I thought you said you always wore your tights to class,' she said. 'You can't do ballet in baggy trousers. Madam Anna likes us all to be very neat and tidy.'

'It's OK,' Christy said. 'I've got tights on underneath.' And he waved cheerfully to Jenny's mum as they drove away.

It wasn't a long drive to the church hall where Madam Anna held her classes, but it seemed very long indeed to Jenny. She looked out of the window all the way so that she didn't have to talk to Christy. She invented conversations with her friends inside her head. 'No, I know I came with him, but I couldn't help it.' 'Poor Jenny – having to come with a boy!' 'A *boy* – isn't it awful?' 'I expect Madam Anna will put him in the little ones' class.' 'Boys *never* know what to do. Fancy your mum telling you to look after him!' By the time Mrs Davis stopped the car Jenny was feeling very sorry for herself, and she was quite certain that all her friends would feel sorry for her too. She grabbed her bag and jumped out of the car, rushing to tell them. As she ran, her tights flopped out of her bag and tangled round her legs ... and Jenny fell flat on her face.

'*Jenny?*'

Jenny scrambled up, and stared. Madam Anna – *Madam Anna!* – was right in front of her.

Jenny dropped her bag and tried to make her greeting curtsy, but as she said, 'Good evening, Madam Anna,' she wobbled and slipped sideways. Her face burnt bright red as she stood up again.

100

'Jenny dear,' Madam Anna said, 'a ballerina does not arrive anywhere in a scrabble and a dash. Now, pick up your tights, and go inside and wash your hands and face.'

Jenny grabbed her bag and her tights and hurried through the door. Her eyes were stinging with angry tears, and her hands and knees were hurting too. It was all that *horrible* boy's fault, she told herself. She had *never* fallen over before. It *had* to be his fault. And she stamped into the changing room and flung herself down on a bench.

'Jenny! Jenny! Guess what! Guess!' Daisy and Sarah and Edna and all her other friends were jumping up and down in excitement. 'Guess what! There's a famous ballerina coming today to see Madam Anna! And guess what else! Her little boy is coming to join *our* class! Unless he's too good, of course, and then he'll go up to the seniors. But a *real* ballerina! She danced with the Royal Ballet, and she was Swanhilda in *Coppélia* and Madam Anna says she was an absol-ute rave!'

Jenny didn't move. She sat on the bench and said nothing at all. The other girls fussed and twittered round her, straightening their tights and smoothing their hair, but Jenny sat still – and thought.

It must be Mrs Davis! Mrs Davis – Christy's mum – was a real ballerina! And she, Jenny – Madam Anna's star dancer – had been rude to her! Had run away from her car! Had been horrid to Christy! Jenny felt as if a whirlwind was rushing about in her head. How would she ever look at Madam Anna again? Oh

101

– if only she could turn time back …

'Jenny! Jenny! Why aren't you getting ready?' Daisy was peering at her.

'Your face is dirty,' Edna said. 'What have you been doing?'

'I fell over,' Jenny said. 'I fell over on my way in.' She didn't say she had been running away from the famous ballerina, but she felt her face grow hot as she thought about it. She got up and went to wash her hands.

'Did you see Madam Anna?' Sarah asked. 'She's waiting outside – this ballerina must be *very* special!'

'What do you think her boy will be like?' Edna did a *pirouette*.

'I expect he'll want to dance with me,' Daisy said, and she smiled at herself in the mirror. Daisy was very pretty, and she was always popular with the boys at school.

'No, he won't,' said Sarah. 'He'll want to dance with Jenny. She's much the best dancer.'

'He'll have to take turns,' said Edna. 'Or it won't be fair.'

'Maybe now one boy's come, lots of others will too,' said Gillie.

'Maybe,' Daisy said, still gazing at herself in the mirror, 'maybe we'll do lifts!'

'WOW!' breathed Edna and Sarah and Gillie.

Jenny, slowly pulling on her tights, felt worse and worse. It sounded as if all the other girls *liked* the idea of Christy joining the class … as if they *wanted* boys to join in. She wriggled into her leotard, and put on her satin slippers.

'You're being very quiet,' Edna told Jenny as she tied her ribbons. 'What's the matter?'

'Nothing,' Jenny said. She was just smoothing her hair when Madam Anna put her head round the door.

'Girls? Girls – come and meet Tara Talliori, formerly prima ballerina of the Royal Ballet. And you must welcome her son, already a dedicated dancer. Now, remember – your *very* best curtsies, *if* you please.'

Daisy and Sarah and Edna and the other girls squeaked and giggled their way out into the hall. Jenny took a deep breath, and followed them …

Madam Anna was standing on the platform at the end of the hall. Beside her was Mrs Davis, and beside Mrs Davis was Christy, neatly dressed in a white T-shirt, black tights and ballet shoes. To Jenny's amazement she saw that Christy was blushing – a deep fiery red creeping up over his face. He looked very uncomfortable indeed, and Jenny found herself feeling sorry for him.

'It must be *horrible* being up there in front of everybody,' she thought, and as she felt more and more sorry for Christy she wished even more that she had been nicer to him.

'Girls,' Madam Anna said, 'we are very lucky this evening. Tara Talliori is going to lead us in our greeting curtsy, and then she will take the class – just for today. I hope you will all be *most* polite and do *exactly* as she tells you.' She turned and smiled at

103

Tara Talliori, and Tara Talliori nodded back.

'Perhaps Christy could join the other students?'
Tara – or Mrs Davis – asked, and Christy jumped
down from the platform so quickly that Jenny was
certain he had been longing and longing to get away.
He hurried down the hall and came to stand next to
Jenny, but he didn't look at her.

Jenny swallowed. There was an uncomfortable
feeling in her throat. She had ignored him all the
way to ballet class; was he going to do the same to
her now?

'Are we ready?' Madam Anna called out, and
she held out her arms. Tara Talliori did the same,
and all the girls copied her. Christy put his hands on
his waist.

'One, two, three – and *down*,' said Madam Anna
... and down they all sank – all except Christy.
Christy bowed a low deep bow, and he bowed
straight at Jenny ... and winked at her ... and
wobbled ... and fell over.

As he scrambled up both he and Jenny began to
laugh. Even when Madam Anna frowned at them
they couldn't stop, and Daisy and Edna and Sarah
and all the other girls began to laugh too ... Tara
Talliori laughed the loudest of all. Even Madam
Anna seemed to be smiling.

As the noise died down Tara Talliori walked
over to the piano. 'Do you mind if I play?' she asked,
and before the pianist could answer, she began to
play a wild and toe-tapping polka.

'Take your partners!' she called out. 'Let's begin

with a warm-up! Remember your posture – and listen to the music!'

There was a moment's complete silence. No class of Madam Anna's had ever begun with a polka … Then Edna and Sarah grabbed each other's hands and began to hop and skip in circles.

Jenny hesitated, and then looked sideways at Christy. He was looking at her, and he took her hand as if it were the most ordinary thing in the world. As they jumped and hopped round the room, it was as if

they had always been friends. Jenny smiled to herself. Maybe boys doing ballet wasn't such a bad thing after all …

And when she and Christy bounced past Madam Anna, and Madam Anna clapped her hands, Jenny was sure of it.

The Hookywalker
Dancers

by Margaret Mahy

In the heart of the great city of Hookywalker was the
School of Dramatic Art. It was full of all sorts of
actors and singers and wonderful clowns, but the
most famous of them all was the great dancer,
Brighton.

Brighton could leap like an antelope and spin
like a top. He was as slender as a needle. In fact, when
he danced you almost expected little stitches to
follow him across the stage. Every day he did his
exercises at the *barre* to music played on his tape-
recorder.

'One and a *plié* and a stretch, two-three, and *port
de bras* and back to first!' he counted. He exercised so
gracefully that, outside the School of Dramatic Art,
pedlars rented ladders so that lovers of the dance
could climb up and look through the window at
Brighton practising.

Of course, life being what it is, many other
dancers were often jealous of him. I'm afraid that

most of them ate too much and were rather fat, whereas Brighton had an elegant figure. They pulled his chair away from under him when he sat down, or tried to trip him up in the middle of his dancing, but Brighton was so graceful he simply made falling down look like an exciting new part of the dance, and the people standing on ladders clapped and cheered and banged happily on the windows.

Although he was such a graceful dancer, Brighton was not conceited. He led a simple life. For instance, he didn't own a car, travelling everywhere on roller skates, his tape-recorder clasped to his ear. Not only this, he did voluntary work for the Society for Bringing Happiness to Dumb Beasts. At the weekends he would put on special performances for pets and farm animals. Savage dogs became quiet as lambs after watching Brighton dance, and nervous sheep grew wool thicker than ever before. Farmers from outlying districts would ring up the School of Dramatic Art and ask if they could hire Brighton to dance to their cows, and many a parrot, temporarily off its seed, was brought back to full appetite by seeing Brighton dance the famous solo called *The Noble Savage in the Lonely Wood.*

Brighton had a way of kicking his legs up that suggested deep sorrow, and his *demi-pliés* regularly brought tears to the eyes of the parrots, after which they tucked into their seed quite ravenously.

One day, the director of the School for Dramatic Art called Brighton to his office.

'Brighton,' he said, 'I have an urgent request

here from a farmer who needs help with a flock of very nervous sheep. He is in despair!'

'Glad to help!' said Brighton in his graceful fashion. 'What seems to be the trouble?'

'Wolves – that's what the trouble is!' cried the director. 'He lives on the other side of the big forest, and a pack of twenty wolves comes out of the forest early every evening and tries to devour some of his prize merinos. It's disturbing the sheep very badly. They get nervous twitches, and their wool is falling out from shock.'

'I'll set off at once,' Brighton offered. 'I can see it's an urgent case.'

'It's a long way,' the director said, doubtfully. 'It's right on the other side of the forest.'

'That's all right,' said Brighton. 'I have my trusty roller skates, and the road is tarred all the way. I'll take my tape-recorder to keep me company, and I'll get there in next to no time.'

'That's very fast,' the director said in a respectful voice. 'Oh, Brighton, I wish all my dancers were like you! Times are hard for the School of Dramatic Art. A lot of people are staying at home and watching car crashes on television. They don't want art – they want danger, they want battle, murder and sudden death – and it's becoming much harder to run the school at a profit. If all our dancers were as graceful as you there would be no problem at all, but as you know a lot of them are just a whisker on the fat side. They don't do their exercises the way they should.'

Little did he realize that the other dancers were

actually listening at the keyhole, and when they heard this critical remark they all began to sizzle with jealousy. You could hear them sizzling with it. 'I'll show him who's fat and who isn't,' muttered a very spiteful dancer called Antoine. 'Where are Brighton's skates?'

Brighton's skates were, in fact, in the cloakroom under the peg on which he hung his beret and his great billowing cape. It was but the work of a moment to loosen one or two vital grommets. The skates looked all right, but they were no longer as safe as skates ought to be.

'There,' said Antoine, laughing nastily. 'They'll hold together for a little bit, but once he gets into the forest they'll collapse, and we'll see how he gets on then, all alone with the wind and the wolves – and without wheels.'

The halls of the School of Dramatic Art rang with the jealous laughter of the other dancers as they slunk off in all directions. A minute later Brighton came in, suspecting nothing, put on his beret and his great billowing cape, strapped on his skates, and set off holding his tape-recorder to his ear.

Now, during the day, the wolves spent a long time snoozing and licking their paws clean in a clearing on top of the hill. From there they had a good view of the Hookywalker road. They could look out in all directions and even see as far as Hookywalker when the air was clear. It happened that their present king was a great thinker, and something was worrying him deeply.

'I know we're unpopular,' sighed the King of the Wolves, 'but what can I do about it? It's the nature of things that wolves steal a few sheep here and there. It's part of the great pattern of nature.' Though this seemed reasonable he was frowning and brooding as he spoke. 'Sometimes – I don't know – I feel there must be more to life than just ravening around grabbing the odd sheep and howling at the moon.'

'Look!' cried the wolf who was on look-out duty. 'Someone is coming down the great road from the city.'

'How fast he's going!' said another wolf. 'And whatever is it he is holding to his ear?'

'Perhaps he has earache,' suggested a female wolf in compassionate tones. None of the wolves had ever seen a tape-recorder before.

'Now then, no feeling sorry for him,' said the King of the Wolves. 'You all know the drill. We get down to the edge of the road, and at the first chance we tear him to pieces. That's all part of the great pattern of nature I was mentioning a moment ago.'

'That'll take his mind off his earache,' said one of the wolves with a fierce, sarcastic snarl.

As the sun set majestically in the west, Brighton, his cloak billowing round him like a private storm cloud, reached the great forest. It was like entering another world, for a mysterious twilight reigned under the wide branches, a twilight without moon or stars. Tall, sombre pines looked down as if they feared the worst. But Brighton skated on, humming to himself. He was listening to the music of *The Noble*

111

Savage and was waiting for one of the parts he liked best. Indeed, so busy was he humming and counting the beats that he did not notice a sudden wobble in his wheels. However, a moment after the wobble, his skates gave a terrible screech and he was pitched into the pine needles by the side of the road.

'Horrakapotchkin!' cried Brighton. 'My poor skates!' (It was typical of this dancer that his first thought was for others.) However, his second thought was of the forest and the wolves that might be lurking there. It occurred to him that they might be tired of merino sheep, and would fancy a change of diet.

'Quick thought! Quick feet!' he said, quoting an old dancing proverb. He rushed around collecting a pile of firewood and pine-cones, and then lit a good-sized fire there on the roadside. It was just as well he did, because when he looked up he saw the forest was alight with fiery red eyes. The wolves had arrived. They stole out of the forest and sat down on the edge of the firelight, staring at him very hard, all licking their lips in a meaningful way.

Brighton did not panic. Quietly, he rewound his tape-recorder to the very beginning, and then stood up coolly and began to do his exercises. A lesser dancer might have started off dancing straight away, but Brighton knew the greatest challenge of his life was ahead of him. He preferred to take things slowly and warm up properly in case he needed to do a few tricky steps before the night was out.

The wolves looked at each other uneasily. The

king hesitated. There was something so tuneful about the music and so graceful about Brighton's dancing that he would have liked to watch it for a bit longer, but he knew he was part of nature's great plan, and must help his pack to tear Brighton to pieces. So he gave the order. 'Charge!'

As one wolf the wolves ran towards Brighton, snarling and growling, but to their astonishment Brighton did not run away. No! He actually ran towards them and then, leaped up in the air – up, up and right over them – his cloak streaming out behind

him. It had the words HOOKYWALKER SCHOOL OF DRAMATIC ART painted on it. The wolves were going so fast that they could not stop themselves until they were well down the road. Brighton, meanwhile, landed with a heroic gesture, wheeled around, and then went on with his exercises, watching the wolves narrowly.

Once again, the wolves charged, and once again Brighton leaped. This time he jumped even higher, and the wolves couldn't help gasping in admiration, much as they hated missing out on any prey.

'Right!' cried the King of the Wolves. 'Let's run round him in ever-decreasing circles.' (This was an old wolf trick.) 'He'll soon be too giddy to jump.' However, being a wolf and not used to classical ballet, the King didn't realize that a good dancer can spin on his toes without getting in the least bit giddy. Brighton spun until he was a mere blur and actually rose several inches in the air with the power of his rotation. It was the wolves who became giddy first; they stumbled over one another, ending up in a heap, with their red eyes all crossed. Finally, they struggled up with their tongues hanging out but they had to wait for their eyes to get uncrossed again.

Seeing they were disabled for the moment by the wonder of his dancing, Brighton now gave up mere jumps and spins and began demonstrating his astonishing technique. Used as he was to dancing for animals, there was still a real challenge about touching the hearts of wolves. Besides, he knew he couldn't go on twirling and leaping high in the air all

114

night. His very life depended on the quality of his dancing. He began with the first solo from *The Noble Savage*. Never in all his life, even at the School of Dramatic Art, had he been more graceful. First, he danced the loneliness of the Noble Savage, and the wolves (though they always travelled in a pack, and were never ever lonely) were so stirred that several of them pointed their noses into the air and howled in exact time to the music. It was most remarkable. Brighton now turned towards the wolves and began to express through dance his pleasure at seeing them. He made it very convincing. Some of the wolves began to wag their tails.

'He's really got something!' said the King of the Wolves. 'This is high-class stuff.' Of course, he said it in wolf language, but Brighton was good at reading the signs and became more poetic than ever before.

'Let me see,' said the King of the Wolves, fascinated. 'With a bit of practice I could manage an act like this myself. I always knew there was more to life than mere ravening. Come on! Let's give it a go!' The wolves began to point their paws and copy whatever movements Brighton made.

Seeing what they were about, Brighton began to encourage them by doing a very simple step and shouting instructions.

'You put your left paw in, you put your left paw out ...'

Of course, the wolves could not understand the words, but Brighton was very clever at mime and they caught on to the idea of things, dancing with great enthusiasm. Naturally, they were not as graceful as Brighton, but then they had not practised for years as he had. Brighton could not help but be proud of them as they began a slow progress down the road back to the city, away from the forest and the sheep on the other side. The moon rose higher in the sky, and still Brighton danced, and the entranced wolves followed him pointing their paws. It was very late at night when they entered the city once more. People going home from the cinema stared and shouted, and pointed (fingers not toes). A lot of them joined in, either dancing or making music on musical instruments – banjos, trombones, combs – or anything that happened to be lying around.

In the School of Dramatic Art, wicked Antoine was just about to dance the very part Brighton usually danced when the sound of the procession made him hesitate. The audience, full of curiosity, left the theatre. Outside was Brighton, swaying with weariness but still dancing, followed by twenty wolves, all dancing most beautifully by now, all in time and all very pleased with themselves, though, it must be admitted, all very hungry.

'Oh,' cried the director of the School of Dramatic Art, rushing out to kiss Brighton on both cheeks. 'What talent! What style! This will save the School of Dramatic Art from extinction.'

'Send out for a supply of sausages,' panted Brighton, 'and write into the wolves' contracts that they will have not only sausages of the best quality, but that their names will appear in lights on top of the theatre. After all, if they are dancing here every night, they won't be able to chase and worry sheep, will they?'

After this, there was peace for a long time, both in the city and out on the farms (where the sheep grew very fat and woolly). The School of Dramatic Art did wonderfully well. People came from miles around to see Brighton and his dancing wolves, and, of course – just as he had predicted – after dancing until late at night, the wolves were too weary to go out ravening sheep. Everyone was delighted (except for the jealous dancers who just sulked and sizzled). Antoine, in particular, had such bad attacks of jealousy that it ruined his digestion and made his stomach rumble loudly, which forced him to abandon ballet altogether. However, Brighton, the wolves, the farmers, the director, and many other people, lived happily ever after in Hookywalker, that great city which people sometimes see looming out of the mist on the fringe of many fairy stories.

A Dream of Sadler's Wells

by Lorna Hill

When Veronica's father dies, suddenly she is uprooted from her life in London and the ballet classes she loves so much. But she makes a new friend caled Sebastian and against all odds continues to practise. Then, at last, she is given the chance to audition for Sadler's Wells ballet school in London ...

A week after Lady Blantosh's Bring and Buy Sale, Aunt June got a typewritten letter from the secretary of the Sadler's Wells School of Ballet saying that my audition was to be on the following Friday. It appeared that Madame had called to see Miss Martin in Newcastle on her way back to London, and between them they had fixed things up.

My thoughts were in a positive whirl, and by the time Thursday came, I was so excited I could neither eat nor sleep. Aunt June had booked a first-class sleeper for me from Newcastle to King's Cross, and I was to be put in special care of the sleeping-car attendant, who in his turn was to get me a porter at the other end of my journey. The porter would get me a taxi, and I was to go straight to Mrs Crapper and stay there until it was time for my audition at twelve o'clock. My ticket had already been bought and was reposing in the little drawer of my dressing-table. Perkins was to take me to the station in the car to catch the night train, which went at ten thirty-five. It was all very simple.

All very simple … How is it that it's always the simple things that turn out to be the most difficult, whereas, when you see breakers ahead, the sea is sure to turn out to be as calm as a millpond?

The Thursday morning dawned grey and misty. Aunt June was going to visit friends at Horchester, ten miles away. She took Perkins with her because of the mist, and promised she'd be back by nine o'clock at the latest so that there'd be plenty of time for Perkins to take me to the station. I was to be all ready to go, she said.

For the umpteenth time I checked over my dancing things – pink tights, black tunic, jock-belt, a pair of blocked and a pair of unblocked canvas practice shoes, a pair of my whitest socks, hairband, hairnet, not to mention plenty of hairgrips. I had washed the tights to make them fit without a wrinkle, as well as for cleanliness, and I'd ironed out the tunic, although I knew I should have to do it again at the other end. It wouldn't be exactly creaseless after it had spent the night in my suitcase! For the umpteenth time I tested the ribbons on my ballet shoes to make sure they were secure, and felt the blocks of my pointe shoes to see that they were hard enough. Lastly, I put into the case unimportant things like my nightie, toothbrush and my brush and comb – just in case I forgot them in the excitement of departure.

Then, on the top of everything, I carefully placed a small parcel wrapped in tissue paper. My mascot! Madame's shoes. Yes, they'd come back from the cleaners that very morning, and they were as good as new. At least, they were quite clean, though Messrs Britelite and Sons carefully explained in a polite little note they'd enclosed in the package that *they* weren't responsible for the worn patches. No, indeed – Covent Garden was responsible for them!

Well, after all this, there was nothing to do but wait as patiently as I could for Aunt June to return.

And all the time the mist grew thicker and thicker …

'I say,' Caroline said, as we came in from the stables at seven o'clock to wash our hands for supper, 'this mist is awful, isn't it? That's the worst of living on the edge of the moors; it comes down from the fells. I do hope –'

She stopped, and a pang of fright shot through me.

'Do hope what?'

'I was going to say I do hope Mummy leaves the Chiswicks' in plenty of time. It'll take Perkins ages to get back.'

I didn't say anything. I was quite sick with fear at the awful thought of missing that train. Surely, surely Fate wouldn't be so unkind as to dash the cup from my lips before I could drink!

At eight o'clock the telephone rang. I dashed to answer it before anyone else could get there. I knew quite certainly that it was about me, and I wanted to hear the worst. When I heard Aunt June's voice at the other end of the wire, I knew that it was indeed the worst!

'Oh, it's you, Veronica,' said the voice, sounding quite cheerful, and not a bit as if my whole future were at stake, 'I'm sorry, dear, about this frightful mist. I'm afraid it's quite impossible for me to get back tonight. Perkins won't risk it – the visibility here is practically nil.'

'But, Aunt June,' I wailed. 'My audition – my audition is tomorrow morning! Have you forgotten? I must – I simply *must* catch the train to London.'

'I'm afraid it's quite impossible, dear,' said the calm voice at the other end. 'We'll arrange another interview for you. It will be quite easy, I'm sure, when we explain. You see, Perkins –'

I put down the receiver, cutting off Aunt June and her maddening voice. 'Arrange another audition for me' – you didn't arrange auditions at a famous school like Sadler's Wells just like that! You were granted an audition, and you turned up for it, by hook or by crook, whether you had a streaming cold, or a splitting headache, whether there was a bus strike and you had to walk, or a pea-soup fog, or – or anything. You let *nothing* stop you! Why – *why* couldn't Aunt June understand? As for Perkins not daring to drive in the mist – I knew quite well that it wasn't Perkins who was afraid but Aunt June …

'What's the matter, Veronica?' said Caroline's anxious voice from behind me. 'Is anything wrong?'

'Wrong?' I repeated. 'It's finished! My career's finished!'

'You mean –?'

'Aunt June can't get back tonight because of the mist,' I said. Then I added bitterly, 'It just doesn't dawn on her that my whole career is at stake.'

'I'm sure she realizes, Veronica,' Caroline put in gently, sticking up for her mother as she sometimes did most unexpectedly. 'It really is frightful outside, you know. I don't think *anyone* could possibly drive in it.'

I dashed away to hide my tears, leaving Caroline looking after me with a worried expression on her face, and Fiona smiling her hateful, knowing smile. I knew that Fiona was pleased that all my hopes were being crushed.

'I must, I *must* do something!' I said to myself. 'What can I do? Oh, God – *please* tell me what to do!'

Then suddenly I had an idea. I expect some people would say God had nothing to do with it – that God was far too busy to bother about a little thing like my dancing, but I was sure in my own mind that my idea was Heaven-sent, and that God was telling me what to do.

I tumbled my things out of my suitcase on to the floor, dashed into the schoolroom and pulled a rucksack from the bottom of the toy cupboard, where now books and tennis rackets and suchlike were kept, dashed back with it to my bedroom and hastily began to repack my things in it. I didn't bother about my nightie and toothbrush, this time, but squeezed in the dancing things as best I could, ending with Madame's shoes. Then, like a shadow, I slipped down the backstairs and out to the stables.

I daren't switch on the electric light for fear someone saw it and began asking questions, so I had to saddle up Arab by the light of my flash lamp. It was much harder than you'd think, but I managed it at last, and led the pony out into the stable yard. I went on leading him, so as to make as little noise as possible. I don't think I need have worried, really – the mist muffled his hooves as effectively as a blanket.

When we reached the long drive, I thought the mist didn't seem to be quite so thick, the reason for which I learned later on. At last I judged it safe to mount, and I did so, my rucksack bulging to bursting-point on my back. It was quite dark, though it was only half past eight and shouldn't have been for a long time yet, but this, I supposed, was owing to the mist.

As I reached the lodge gates, I wondered what Sebastian was doing – we hadn't seen him since the morning. And then, just as I drew level with the cottage, a voice said: 'Halt! Your money or your life! This is Daredevil Dick of the roving eye and the ready hand!'

I gave a gasp.

'Oh, Sebastian! You did give me a shock! I was

just thinking about you.'

'Well, in that case I oughtn't to have given you a shock, ought I?' he laughed. 'I was just coming up to the Hall to see what had happened about the mist. I imagined they'd have got you into town ages ago. And by the way, "where are you going to, my pretty maid" at this time of night, if you don't mind my asking?'

My thoughts flashed back to a day, more than a year ago now – a morning in July when I'd been perched on the top of this very gate, and Sebastian's voice had asked almost the same question. I gave the same answer now. I said: 'I'm running away. I am really! I'm not joking. You see …'

Then out it all came. Aunt June's visit to Horchester; the mist; my audition. Of course, Sebastian knew all about that.

'So you see,' I ended, 'I've just *got* to go – mist or no mist.'

'But, Veronica, you *can't* go,' Sebastian said, his voice sounding anxious and tense. 'You couldn't possibly, you know. You'd never get there in time, anyway.'

'Of course I know I can't catch *that* train,' I argued. 'But there'll be another one – a mail train or a milk train early in the morning. There are trains to London all the time. There must be one; there *must*! My audition isn't till twelve. I might just get there. Anyway, I'm going to have a jolly good try – they say you can do anything if you really make up your mind to it.' I kicked Arab sharply, and we shot off into the mist. Fortunately the gates had been left open for Aunt June and Perkins. I felt pretty sure Sebastian wouldn't have opened them for me!

'Veronica!' came Sebastian's voice out of the mist. 'Don't be an idiot – you don't know what you're taking on – honestly you don't. The mist is nothing here to what it'll be when you get away from the trees. It's never so thick where there are trees. There are no buses, you know. This isn't a market day –'

'You said that a year ago, I remember!' I said with an excited laugh. 'Well, I shall *ride* to Newcastle if necessary. I don't care! I shall get there somehow. Goodbye!'

But I had reckoned without the mist. As Sebastian had said, the moment Arab and I left the trees it closed round us like muffling folds of cotton wool. A figure loomed up beside us and caught hold of Arab's bridle. Sebastian again! I might have known he wouldn't be so easily shaken off.

'Veronica – you've *got* to stop! I order you to stop!'

'You take your hand away from my bridle, or I'll – I'll ...' I raised my crop threateningly, though I didn't really mean to strike him with it.

Then suddenly Sebastian let go. With a gasp of relief, and not a little of astonishment, I saw him vanish into the mist, and I was once more alone. I say 'with relief' but really it was with rather mixed feelings that I saw him go – he seemed to be my last friend in a nightmare world. But I set my teeth and

determined not to give in. I *must* get there somehow,
I told myself – mist or no mist. The audition –
Sadler's Wells – my beloved dancing career …

Thoughts raced round in my head as I urged Arab onwards.

Strange noises came from all round me. Then I realized that they were only the sounds of the country-side – sounds you don't notice in broad daylight with the sun shining – a cow coughing, or blowing down its nose on the far side of the hedge; an owl screeching; the metallic whirr of a grouse rising in alarm out of a nearby thicket. It was terribly eerie and queer. My heart began to beat quickly and I wished that Sebastian hadn't given in like that and gone away. It would have been a comfort to have had his company, even if he *had* argued all the time.

Then, out of the mist, came a familiar sound behind me – the sound of a horse trotting.

A thrill of fright went through me. I was being pursued! I thought of all the people Sebastian might have told about me running away. His father, Uncle Adrian; then I remembered Sebastian saying that he was away. Uncle John – but he'd rung up to say he'd be staying in town for the night, as he always did if there was a mist. Trixie – she certainly couldn't ride on horseback. Pilks, Dickson. Neither could they – certainly not in a mist like this! It could only be Sebastian himself. Perhaps he thought he had more chance of stopping me when he was mounted. Well, he'd see! I drew in to the side of the road and waited for the rider to come up with me – I knew by the way he was trotting that I hadn't the ghost of a chance of escaping by speed, not being able to do more than a very slow walk myself.

'That you, Veronica?' came Sebastian's voice after a few minutes. 'I thought you couldn't have got far.'

'If you think you're going to stop me ...' I began desperately. 'If you think –'

'Stop being melodramatic, my dear cousin-sort-of,' said Sebastian in his usual bantering tones, 'and let's get going! We'll have to step on the gas – and how! – if you mean to catch your milk train – if there *is* a milk train.'

'You don't mean that you're coming with me?' I said with a thrill of joy and hope.

'I certainly *do* mean it,' said Sebastian. 'Nothing else to be done as far as I can see – or rather I should say *feel*. More accurate! I always know when I'm beaten, and I could tell by the sound of your voice just now that nothing short of prison bars would stop you from venturing into the wild. Well, as I haven't any prison bars handy, the only thing to do is to come along with you myself and see you don't exceed the speed limit! I said to myself: "The girl's quite determined – obvious she can't go by herself. Get lost for one thing; take the wrong turning; get run over most likely. Anyway, certainly wouldn't get anywhere – not in this mist, being a Cockney brat." So I had to do the Boy Scout stunt. Can't let a fellow *artiste* down, if you see what I mean. This is my good deed for today!'

'Sebastian, you're a *brick*!' I said, trying not to burst out crying for joy and relief. 'As you say, "let's get going".'

To be caught in a mist at night on a moorland road in Northumberland doesn't sound so dreadful, but you try it! I was quite hardened to the London fogs when you could only see a few inches in front of your nose, but in London you were at least among other people. There were lighted shops on all sides to cheer you, even if you *could* only see them dimly, as if through smoked glass. There were kindly policemen at crossings and corners, doing all they could to help you; there was noise, and bustle, and the friendly Underground where you could nearly forget about the fog outside. But here, on this lonely road, with the unseen hills wrapped in cloud all around you, the silence was intense. The only sounds that broke it were the occasional prattle of a moorland stream as it tumbled over its stony bed, or the plaintive cry of a peewit or a curlew.

The moorland road was unfenced and at first I'd been terrified for fear my pony strayed off the path on to the endless open moor that stretched away on every side. But I found that Sebastian knew exactly what to do about that – he just let Warrior have his head and Warrior kept to the road all right. He hadn't been born and bred on the Northumbrian moors for nothing! I found that Arab was just as wise. Our only worry was knowing which way to go when we came to a fork, or a crossroads. Fortunately Sebastian had brought his torch, which saved the situation. Although several times he had to climb the signposts to get near enough to flash the light on to the names, we did at least know we were going in the right direction.

'It's a good thing you brought that torch, Sebastian,' I said, after one of our many stops. 'I had one too, but I left it in the stable. I never thought of bringing it with me.'

'No, I rather guessed you wouldn't,' said Sebastian with laughter in his voice. 'All you would think of bringing would be a pair of ballet shoes and some tights! Not much use for a night out in the mist!'

I blushed guiltily in the dark, when I remembered how carefully I had packed Madame's precious shoes into my rucksack, not bothering to bring a brush and comb, or even a nightie! Sebastian came perilously near the truth!

'I wonder what they thought when they found I'd gone?' I said suddenly. 'Trixie, and Caroline, and all of them. Oh, Sebastian – I quite forgot to leave a note to explain! How dreadful of me! Do you think they'll be awfully worried?'

'Oh, no – shouldn't think so,' said Sebastian. 'I expect they'll say: "Oh, well – that's the end of her", shut the door and go to bed. "No need to worry; people disappear every day." ' Then I think he sensed how upset I really was at what I had done – or rather what I had *not* done, for his teasing tone changed and he said seriously: 'It's OK, Veronica! I left a letter to my father telling him what had happened. He'll get it when he comes back from the village. I think he'll agree that it was the only thing to do – sensible chap, my father! By the way –' He stopped suddenly.

'Yes – what?'

'Well, you remember when we were discussing our Matric results the other day?'

'Yes, what about it?'

'Well, you remember when Fiona said something about me *needing* to do well because of my career. She said: "You'll have to be pretty clever if you're going to be a barrister." And I said: "Yes – *if* I'm going to be a barrister."'

'Yes,' I said. 'I remember.'

'The fact is,' went on Sebastian, the excitement in his voice making it wobble a little, 'the fact is, Veronica, it's definitely fixed, and I'm *not* going in for Law. I had it out with my father the other day, and I'm going to make Music my career. You're the very first person to know.'

'Oh, Sebastian, I'm so glad!' I exclaimed. 'I know what it's like to want to do something most awfully and have everyone against you.'

'When all came to all,' continued Sebastian, 'Father said he'd half suspected the truth. He said that no one could remain totally oblivious of the fact that my heart was in the piano, judging by the number of hours I spend sitting at it! I *have* practised rather a lot these hols,' he added apologetically. 'In fact I've done nothing else – except ride with you lot now and then. Well, my father agreed that it was no earthly good my taking up Law as a profession if my heart was set on other things, so I'm to try for a scholarship to the Royal College of Music next year.

He really was most awfully decent about it – he's an understanding chap is my father. If I get the scholarship I'm coming to London to study, so you'll be able to come to the Albert Hall with me, and I'll go to Covent Garden with you, what!'

After this there was silence between us for a long time. We were each far too deep in our own thoughts to talk. It was a good thing our thoughts were blissful, because the outlook was anything but cheerful. 'Outlook' is quite the wrong word, really, because we couldn't see anything at all now – not even the ditches at the sides of the road. If it hadn't been for the wonderful sixth sense of our ponies we'd have been blundering into them at every step. The mist seemed to get thicker and thicker, and we got colder and colder.

'This is the top of the road over Cushat's Crag, you know,' said Sebastian, breaking the long silence. 'I shouldn't be surprised if the mist isn't at its worst here. It usually is. If the mist is rolling off the hills, as it is tonight, and not rising off the low ground – well, you're right in the middle of the clouds up here. When we get over the top and go down the other side it may thin out a bit.'

'How many miles have we come?' I asked. 'We seem to have been riding for hours and hours.'

'About ten miles,' said Sebastian. Then he flashed his torch on to his wristwatch. 'It's half past eleven, so it's taken us two hours. We have another twenty miles to go to get to Newcastle. When we get on to the Military Road that runs along the Roman

133

Wall, we might come across a garage. There's one at the crossroads – at least I *think* it's a garage, but it may only be a filling station. We might knock them up and get a taxi – at least we might if the mist lifts a bit. I'm pretty sure they wouldn't turn out in this, no matter what we offered them. We'll have to get a lift somehow, you know, and hang the expense! You won't be fit for anything tomorrow after this.'

'Oh, yes I shall,' I said, trying to stop my teeth chattering. 'B-ballet dancers are pretty t-tough.'

'Hello! What's this?' exclaimed Sebastian, reining in Warrior. 'Golly! A covered-in bus stop. What a find! Let's stop here and rest the ponies for a bit, shall we?'

We tethered the ponies to an iron railing that stretched away into the mist on either side of the tiny shelter, and sank down thankfully on the hard wooden seat inside. Once more Sebastian flashed on his torch, and I saw by its light that he had swung round his rucksack and was taking something out of it – a Thermos flask and a packet of sandwiches.

'I told you once before that I always carry my own canteen about with me, didn't I?' he said. 'Brainwave, what! It was a good thing Bella had just made the coffee and stood it on the stove to keep hot. I'd like to have been there when she found it gone. She wouldn't even be able to blame the cat – not with hot coffee! I'm afraid I made a bad job of the sandwiches. Hadn't much time, you see, and I couldn't find anything to go in them, except cheese.'

'It tastes like caviare!' I laughed. 'I mean, just as

wonderful.'

'I hope not!' Sebastian said solemnly. 'Personally I loathe caviare. Filthy stuff!'

'Oh, I love it,' I said. 'Jonathan always had it when he sold a picture and threw a party!'

'It's a good thing we don't all like the same things,' pronounced Sebastian. 'I'll have the ice-cream, and you can have the caviare.'

'Oh, but I like ice-cream, too!'

'Well, what *don't* you like?'

I thought long and deeply. Finally I said: 'Tripe.'

'Don't like it either,' laughed Sebastian. 'So what?'

'Deadlock, I'm afraid,' I said. 'I seem to be frightfully easy to please. I like simply everything. Oh, no – I've just thought of something I simply *loathe* – caraway seeds!'

'Love 'em!' declared Sebastian. 'So the situation is saved at the eleventh hour. You can have my caviare, and I'll have your caraway seeds!'

We stayed quite a long time in the shelter so as to give the ponies a good rest – and ourselves too. When at last we decided it was time to move, it was twelve o'clock.

'The witching hour!' exclaimed Sebastian as we rode off. 'Now is the time for hobgoblins, witches, earthbound spirits, and every sort of uncanny thing to be abroad!'

'Ugh!' I said. 'Don't! You make me feel creepy! The mist is uncanny enough – without your ghostly et ceteras!'

For ages and ages we rode onwards, and the silence between us grew longer as we grew more and more weary. Arab was beginning to stumble and Warrior's trot had lost its springy sound. We walked the ponies quite a lot of the time.

'I wonder where we are now?' I said, with a sigh of utter weariness. 'It seems hours and hours since we left that bus stop.'

'It is,' answered Sebastian. 'Two, anyway ... Gosh! D'you see what's happened? The mist is thinning. I can see that signpost clearly. We're coming to the crossroads I told you about. Now for our garage!'

But alas! The garage proved to be a mere filling station as Sebastian had feared. It was as black and dead-looking as the dodo.

'The chappie probably lives miles away,' Sebastian said. 'It's no use our trying to ferret him out, because we don't know in which direction the nearest village is. Of course we might go back and try Simonburn –'

'Oh, let's *not*,' I said. 'Simonburn is the other way to Newcastle, isn't it? I don't want to go back – I want to go *on*!'

We went on. We passed an AA box, with a telephone inside, but alas! it was no use to us as we hadn't a key.

'A friend of mine lives somewhere about here,' said Sebastian after a bit. 'Or rather his father does. His name is Dillon – Jack Dillon – and they have a farm hereabouts. Ah, I thought so! Here it is – Hunter's Copse.' He stopped in the middle of the road and flashed his torch so that I could read the name on the gate.

'Look out!' I yelled. 'There's something coming!' It was a car, judging by the two pale lights gleaming through the fog. To my surprise Sebastian flung himself off Warrior's back, and leapt into the middle of the road, waving his arms wildly and yelling at the top of his voice.

'Stop! Stop! Hi – wait a minute!'

Fortunately the driver had good eyesight and was going at a snail's pace. He stopped at once, let down the window of the car and yelled back: 'What's that? You in any trouble?'

'You've said it!' yelled back Sebastian. 'Half a mo' and we'll tell you about it. You can help us a lot if you will. Filthy night, isn't it?'

'Filthy?' said the man in the car. 'I could find a better name for it than that! Are you two youngsters alone?'

'Yes,' said Sebastian. 'That is, we've got our ponies, of course. You see …' There, on that foggy and deserted road in the wilds of Northumberland, with a bit of help from me, he told our story – all about the Bring and Buy Sale, Madame, my audition at Sadler's Wells, and finally the last awful catastrophe – Aunt June and the mist. I expect it sounded a bit fantastic. Anyway, when we'd finished, the man whistled and said in an awestruck voice: 'My holy godfathers! And you two have ridden on a couple of ponies all the way from Bracken to here, and you are prepared to do another twenty miles or so to Newcastle, in order to catch a hypothetical train to London. My sainted aunt!'

'We *did* hope you would give us a lift, sir,' said Sebastian hopefully.

'A lift?' said the man. 'I should just say I could! But look here – I can get you two in the back all right but how about the animals? I doubt if they'd go in the boot! Do we tow them, or what? No doubt you have ideas! You don't seem lacking in ingenuity!'

'I have a friend who lives at this farm,' Sebastian explained, waving in the direction of the gateway on our right. 'We could leave the ponies here and I could collect them tomorrow morning. The mist'll have cleared off by then, and I could ride them back all right – I mean ride one and lead the other.'

'But, Sebastian,' I expostulated, 'won't your friend object to being knocked up at two o'clock in the morning?'

Sebastian laughed shortly.

'I should just say he would! We needn't disturb him, though. As a matter of fact the farm is a couple of miles off the road, but I happen to know that this field is pasture' – he flashed his torch on to the short grass inside the gate to reassure me – 'and the animals will be quite OK. I'll be back to collect them before he even knows they're there!'

'Well, that's an idea, certainly,' said the man in the car. 'You two do the doings, and I'll have a smoke meantime. The night's young! I ought to have been in Newcastle before midnight, but now it's of no account when I get there. May as well be hung for a sheep as a lamb!'

He flicked open his lighter, and I saw his eyes. They reassured me, being all crinkly round the edges, as if he laughed a lot. I breathed a sigh of relief. Being town bred, I felt it was a bit risky to go making friends with strangers in the middle of a moor at two o'clock in the morning!

As I fondled Arab's warm, silky neck before setting him free, I suddenly realized that I was saying a long goodbye to my pony. If I was accepted as a pupil of the Wells School I shouldn't be coming back here until the holidays, and who knew what might happen to Arabesque? Aunt June would most probably send him back to his owner at Merlingford, and I would see him no more. A tear stole down my nose at the thought of it.

'Come on! What are you waiting for?' said Sebastian's voice at my elbow. 'We're all ready, aren't we? I'll dump the tack in this spinney – I certainly don't feel like taking it with us to Newcastle – I should have to cart it all the way back tomorrow. Just shine the light, will you?'

I held the torch whilst Sebastian climbed the railings into a little copse that lay between the field and the road on one side of the gate. He pushed the saddles and bridles under a thick tangle of blackberry bushes, and piled bracken on top of them.

'Nobody will know they're there,' he declared

when he had finished. 'Only hope it doesn't rain really hard, that's all!'

We went back to the car and got inside. Never had a car felt so warm and luxurious as that old and battered Ford Eight – not even Aunt June's palatial Rolls! We sank down on the imitation leather cushions with a sigh of thankfulness, feeling that the worst of our long trek was over.

We got to Newcastle Central Station at exactly half past four, the mist having thinned considerably as we drove eastwards. We learned that there was a train to London at a quarter to six, so Sebastian led the way to the one and only buffet which was open all night, and procured two large, thick cups of steaming hot coffee and a plate of doorstep sandwiches. Ordinarily we might have turned up our noses at them, but after our ordeal we were only too thankful to get a hot drink and something to eat. When we had finished, we went to the general waiting room. There were several people sitting or lying on the seats and quite a few slumped over the centre table, fast asleep, their heads on their arms. Sebastian found the woman who was in charge of the place, and tipped her to wake us up in time for the London train. Then we lay down on an empty bench, our heads at opposite ends like a couple of sardines. Sebastian had taken off his coat and he covered us both with it. We used our rucksacks for pillows because the bench was made of wood and was pretty hard to lie on. I must add that I removed my pointe shoes (and Madame's) from the rucksack before I lay on it for fear I squashed them!

'Goodnight, Veronica,' Sebastian said with a yawn. 'We managed it OK, didn't we?'

'Oh, Sebastian,' I said, half to myself. 'You *are* sweet!'

'What's that?' asked Sebastian sleepily.

'Oh, nothing,' I answered, knowing by past experience that under no circumstances must you call a boy 'sweet'! 'Goodnight!'

◉

Fortunately the train started from Newcastle, so it was punctual. There were no sleepers on it, even if I had the necessary cash, which I hadn't, but Sebastian managed to hire me a rug and a pillow. How he did it I don't know, but I was full of gratitude and admiration. I couldn't help thinking of the time when I had held the view that people who lived in Northumberland were next door to savages. Sebastian knew a great deal more about travelling than I did – there was no denying the fact.

'Mind you get a taxi straight to the school,' he said as the guard began slamming carriage doors. 'And don't forget the address – 45 Colet Gardens, Baron's Court.'

'As if I should!' I laughed. 'Why, it's written on my heart!'

'So long, Veronica!' he yelled, as the train began to slide away from the platform. 'Good luck!'

'Goodbye!' I yelled back. 'And thank you for everything!'

141

His face swam in a mist before my eyes, and I realized that I was no longer laughing – I was crying! It wasn't only leaving Sebastian behind that made me cry, but all the other things too – Arabesque, the moors, Caroline, Bracken Hall itself. I realized, too late, that I hadn't even said a proper goodbye to them.

As the train got up speed, I lay down on the seat and tried to sleep, but the carriage wheels seemed as if they were turning in my head, and the melody they played was the *Holberg Suite*. My heart had a queer feeling – as if someone was slowly squeezing it – a feeling I hadn't had for a very long time; in fact, not since that journey north more than a year ago. How odd, I thought, that on that occasion I had been homesick for the noisy Underground and all the sounds and sights of London. Now my heart was aching for the moors and woods of Northumberland!

The Holberg Suite changed to *The Dance of the Sugar Plum Fairy*, then to *Les Sylphides*, and finally the whirring of the wheels merged into the unearthly music of Tchaikovsky's *Swan Lake*. I slept at last.

The train was only a quarter of an hour late. I learned from some well-informed passengers that the fog had lifted as soon as we had left Darlington behind, and the train had made up time on the southern part of the journey. It was half past eleven when I dashed through the barrier at King's Cross and made for the taxi rank. There was a touch on my arm.

'Veronica!'

I turned in surprise; then gave a gasp of joy. There in front of me was a well-known figure, towering above the other passengers – a young man with a shock of unruly black hair, and a little black beard.

'Jonathan! Whatever are you doing here?'

'It looks as if I'm meeting *you*!' he laughed.

'But how did you –' I began.

'Look,' said Jonathan, taking my arm and hurrying me along. 'D'you mind if we leave the explanations until we're in the taxi – we'll have to get moving, you know, if we're to get to Baron's Court by twelve o'clock. And I expect you'll need a few spare minutes to get ready –' He whirled me along and into the taxi.

'Five minutes will do!' I laughed, as I sank on to the seat. 'Oh, Jonathan, it *is* good to see you! I was feeling dreadfully homesick, but now it's as though I've come home instead! But please, will you explain how you knew I was on that train. I didn't know I was going to be on it myself until half past five this morning.'

'Just a moment,' said Jonathan. 'Mrs Crapper, the dear old soul, said I was to give you this, and to be sure you drank it' – he pulled a Thermos flask out of his pocket. 'She said she was sure you wouldn't have had any breakfast. Have you?'

'Well, no – I haven't,' I confessed.

'Get on with these then,' went on Jonathan, producing a packet of sandwiches out of the other pocket. 'You've only a few minutes. Well, now for the explanation. At a most uncivilized hour in the morning – six-thirty to be exact – I was roused from my downy pillow by a long-distance telephone call. It was from a friend of yours way up north – a young man, I guessed, from the voice.'

'Sebastian!' I gasped, pausing with a sandwich halfway to my mouth. 'He isn't a young man; he's a boy, and my cousin. At least a sort of a cousin. But how did he find your number? I never told it to him – in fact I don't know it myself. At least I did, but I've forgotten it.'

'Well, I'm as much in the dark there as you are!' laughed Jonathan. 'All I can suggest is that he knew my address and badgered the exchange until they looked up my number.'

'Oh, he'd do that all right!' I exclaimed. 'Trust Sebastian!'

'Anyway, he got me all right,' went on Jonathan. 'And he told me the tale, and here I am, half asleep through being robbed of my beauty sleep, but willing! And by the way, Veronica – congratulations!'

'Keep them till afterwards!' I said, finishing off the coffee. 'They may think I'm frightful and turn me away. Gosh! Here we are. Oh, Jonathan – I feel *awful*!'

'Keep your pecker up!' said Jonathan. 'I'll be waiting for you with the taxi at the corner. Best of luck!'

At exactly twelve o'clock I walked into the studio where I'd been told my audition would take place.

My hair was neatly fastened in the net, my tights pulled up, and the creases in my tunic smoothed out as much as possible. I had a queer feeling in my inside, like when you dive off the high spring-board at the swimming baths for the first time, and my legs felt as if they belonged to somebody else. My hour had come – the hour I had thought of, and dreamed of for so long. I could hardly believe it.

The audition wasn't really so terrifying after all. Only a pretty fair-haired lady and a quiet gentleman with sad, dark eyes that looked as if they saw through you, and far beyond you, and yet made you feel at home just the same. I learned afterwards that usually part of the audition takes place in an ordinary class, but Madame had managed to get me one all to myself because the school hadn't yet started after the holidays.

While I was doing some *grands-jetés* the door of the studio opened and another gentleman looked in. He watched me for a moment, and then said: 'Come! You can spring higher than that! Try again!'

I was very tired, but he didn't know that, of course, and I certainly wasn't going to tell him, because that would have looked like making excuses for myself. I made up my mind to jump higher than I had ever done before – somehow he made me want to do it.

'Good!' he said approvingly. 'I knew you could! Your elevation is excellent. You've got a nice line, too.'

Then suddenly I recognized him. He was the

temperamental ballet master I had watched the day I'd gatecrashed. And here he was being quite friendly! With a smile and a nod he shut the door again, and went away.

When I had done all they asked, the lady told me to take off my socks. She examined my feet most carefully, asking me all sorts of questions as to whether I had ever had any trouble with my feet, whether they ever ached, whether I had ever sprained either of my ankles, all of which I answered truthfully in the negative. Finally she murmured: 'Very nice!' told me I could put on my socks again, and go.

'Please – *please!*' I begged. 'Is it all right? Can I come? Of course I expect it's all against the rules, but couldn't you – couldn't you just tell me if I can come?'

The gentleman looked at the lady and they both smiled.

'Well,' said the gentleman, 'it *is* a little – shall we say unusual, but I think we can put you out of your misery. If you really think you'll be happy here, and don't mind the hard work, well, yes – you shall come.'

'Oh, *thank you!*' I said. 'I know I shall be happy. When your dream comes true, you're bound to be happy, aren't you? And as for work – I'll – I'll work my fingers to the bone ...' I stopped suddenly, realizing that this was rather a funny way to put it when one was referring to ballet! 'I mean, I'll do the very best I can if you'll let me work here.'

'That is all that is necessary,' said the lady, writing something in a book. 'And now I expect you'll want to be going? The secretary will write to your aunt about times and so on. Term begins on Monday and you'll be in the Junior class.' Then she looked at me rather hard, and added: 'You look tired, dear. Were you very excited about your audition?'

'Yes,' I said, 'but not as excited as I would have been if it hadn't been for missing the train last night.' Then out it all came – Aunt June's visit, my flight from Bracken Hall, and my encounter with Sebastian. As I talked, I realized how unbelievable it must all sound, here in civilized London, with the Underground, and the buses, not to mention taxis at every street corner, all taking you wherever you wanted to go at a moment's notice.

'And then the car came along,' I finished, 'and that was the end of our adventure – except that Sebastian will have to collect the ponies this morning and ride them all that way back – twenty miles, at least.'

'A real friend in need – that young man!' said the quiet gentleman. Then he murmured something to the lady about the grit and tenacity of these North Country children. 'And, after all, it's what we need,' he added. 'That, along with other qualities.'

'Oh, but it was Sebastian who was tenacious,' I said quickly. 'I'd never have managed it if it hadn't been for him. You don't *know* how marvellous he was!'

'I think there was grit on both sides,' declared the gentleman with a smile. 'I'm glad to see that you don't easily give up, my dear, when you make up your mind to do a thing.'

And that was the end of my audition. As I left the building, I looked back and gave a sigh of happiness:

45 COLET GARDENS – SADLER'S WELLS SCHOOL OF BALLET.

My dream had come true!

Ballet for Drina

by Jean Estoril

Drina's parents died when she was very young and now she lives with her grandparents. She has everything a girl could ask for, but when they move to London, to her horror Drina is told that she is no longer allowed to dance, and dancing is what Drina likes to do best ...

Nothing much was said that evening before Drina went to bed, and, as a matter of fact, she went to bed very early. She was heavy and headachy after the emotional afternoon, so Mrs Chester packed her off and brought her hot milk when she was undressed.

'Now don't lie there thinking about things. Get a good sleep. You're going to have your wish, and there's no further need to worry.'

'I'll try, Granny,' Drina said meekly, and she drank the milk and curled up contentedly in her narrow bed. She slept almost at once and Big Ben was striking nine before she awoke.

After breakfast Mrs Chester said: 'Why don't

you go out for a brisk walk this morning? It's a lovely day, though very cold.'

So Drina put on her hat and coat and the big fur-lined gloves that had been one of her grandfather's Christmas presents. She took her purse, too, just in case she came back past any bookshops.

She paused for a short while on Westminster Bridge, but the wind was too cold for lingering. So she returned to the Embankment and strode rapidly towards Waterloo Bridge, her heavy hair blown back from her face and her cheeks beginning to glow.

Seagulls wheeled and cried over the grey water, reminding her suddenly and vividly of the coasts of Wester Ross and the Lleyn Peninsula, where there had been so many seabirds. Perhaps, next summer, she would ask to be taken back to one of them.

She walked so fast that she had soon reached Waterloo Bridge, and she turned towards the Strand, with some idea of making her way back to Trafalgar Square and then across St James's Park. But she had not gone far when she caught sight of a poster and the words 'Royal Opera House' sprang out at her. It was a programme for the current season. A moment's study showed her that there would be opera that night, but the next evening there was ballet … a wonderful programme. Ballet at Covent Garden on New Year's Eve!

Drina stood stock-still on the crowded pavement, and a little man, pushing past her, said amiably enough: 'Nar then! Nar then! Bin struck all of a heap?'

It was true enough, too. Drina had been struck by a daring idea. In her purse she had her Christmas money. Was there the faintest hope that, if she went to the Royal Opera House, she might get two seats for the ballet? If she *did* manage to get them, then surely her grandmother would go with her – now?

But there probably wasn't any hope at such a late date, though she had heard her grandfather speak of getting 'returns'. 'Returns' were tickets that people handed back at the last moment, because they had found they couldn't use them.

Her heart was beating wildly by this time, and her hands were clammy with excitement and hope. She had never seen the Royal Opera House, but was sure that it was not far away from where she stood.

A policeman was standing on the corner and she retraced her steps to ask hesitantly: 'Please can you tell me the way to the Royal Opera House?'

The policeman looked down at her, smiling. 'Want to go to the opera?'

'No, the ballet,' Drina said earnestly.

'Well, cross over and keep straight on up Wellington Street. You'll soon see it on your left.'

'Oh, thanks awfully!' And Drina waited till the traffic stopped and bounded over the crossing. But as she continued up Wellington Street she walked more and more slowly. Just now, not knowing whether she would get seats or not, she could savour the hope. In five minutes she might have no hope at all, and suddenly she was on fire with eagerness to see the Royal Ballet and the greatest of all ballerinas.

Crossing a side street she slipped on a cabbage leaf and almost fell and she thought that the Royal Opera House was not in a very nice neighbourhood. But its very situation in the heart of the market, as it seemed, somehow began to add an extra aura of romance, and when she saw the huge building in front of her, her heart quickened, though her footsteps did not.

There was a notice saying 'Box Office' by a side door and a few people were going in and out. Drina, suddenly very shy and extremely doubtful of herself, pushed open the door and found herself in warm gloom. It was the first time she had tried to book theatre seats and she began to feel small and very young.

There were three people in front of her at the booking-office, the window of which was very high, so high that Drina wondered if she would be able to see over the top when she got closer. A tall, prosperous-looking man was putting down several pound notes to pay for seats in the Grand Tier and Drina envied him and his party fiercely. Lucky, lucky people, who were sure to see *Les Sylphides, Daphnis and Chloe* and *Les Patineurs* the following night!

The man immediately in front of her was paying for the Grand Tier, too. Drina stared blankly into the middle of his back and tried to will the cheerful man in the box office to find her two seats.

It was her turn and she stood on tiptoe, looking up at him. At first, in her intense eagerness, no words would come, then she gasped out: 'Oh, please, I suppose you haven't – are there *any* seats for tomorrow night?'

'How many do you want?'

'Oh, two.'

Though she had nerved herself to hear the words: 'No, I'm sorry. There aren't any seats!' they did not come. The young man's face disappeared, and she stood stiffly on tiptoe, her hand, clutching the purse, resting on the edge of the high ledge.

After what seemed a long time, the young man's face was back again.

'The only seats there are,' he said, 'are two in the Stalls Circle. They're rather at the side … you'll have a slightly restricted view. But they're all I have.' He named the price, and Drina gasped with relief. She had enough money.

'Oh, thank you! I'll take them.' Drina could hardly believe in her good luck. She paid, took the small envelope marked 'Royal Opera House', and stumbled out into the cold sunshine again. Among the cabbage leaves some way down the street, she stopped to examine the tickets.

She was going to see the Royal Ballet … first class ballet for the very first time. She was going to see the inside of that famous opera house; the great staircase, the glittering chandeliers, that she had so far known only from pictures in ballet books.

She put the tickets away in her purse and somehow got herself down the Strand. She had enough sense to dive down the steps and cross Trafalgar Square underground. Otherwise, in her dazed state, she would probably have got run over and would never have seen the ballet at all.

She arrived back at the flat starry-eyed and almost incoherent with excitement. She babbled so much that Mrs Chester said quite gently: 'Now start again, Drina! I haven't grasped it yet. What ballet have you got tickets for?'

'Oh, Granny, for the Royal Ballet tomorrow night at Covent Garden! I just can't believe it! Oh, Granny, you *will* come with me? I shall die if you won't.'

Mrs Chester said dryly: 'There's no need to die, Drina. Since you've been lucky enough to get seats of course I'll come. It's a good thing that you've got that new party dress. We shall need to dress up.'

'And Grandfather won't mind, will he? I only had enough money for two tickets, and, anyway, there weren't any more seats.'

'No, I don't suppose he'll mind. As a matter of fact he rang up yesterday evening to try and get seats for us, but there were none at all then. You must have got "returns". What a lucky girl you are!'

So Drina was in seventh heaven and her grandmother sighed because she could get so little sense out of her for the rest of the day.

Drina scarcely knew how she would live until it was time to go to the ballet, but Mrs Chester was determined to keep her occupied. In the morning they went shopping and in the afternoon they went to the wintry Zoo, where Drina forgot a little of her restless excitement in watching the antics of the monkeys and the strange writhings of the snakes in the Reptile House.

The Zoo closed early, of course, so they returned to the West End and had tea, returning to the flat in good time to dress for the theatre.

Drina's new dress was white and stiff. It was quite the most grown-up dress she had ever had. To add to her feeling of elegance she had a little scarlet stole to put round her shoulders and a small scarlet evening bag to hold her handkerchief and comb.

Mr Chester took them to Covent Garden in the car, but pointed out that they would have to come back by taxi, as he had no idea what time the ballet would be over. Drina sat alone in the back of the car, warmly wrapped up in her best coat and a fluffy rug, and, as she looked out at the evening glitter of London, she could hardly believe that she was really Drina Adams on her way to see the Royal Ballet.

Mr Chester drew up in front of the Opera House, in the midst of all the arriving and departing taxis, and Drina caught glimpses of figures in evening dress.

'Have a good time!' called Mr Chester, as he began to drive away, and Mrs Chester led Drina firmly inside, into the glare of lights and the company of crowds of laughing, chattering people. She seemed to know her way about very well and led Drina quickly round the back of the auditorium to the cloakroom.

'Oh, Granny, you've been before!' Drina said breathlessly, trying to take in the vast building.

'Of course I have. Hurry up and take your coat off, Drina. There's going to be a crowd in here very soon.'

So Drina handed her coat and gloves to the attendant and combed her hair. Then she arranged the stole and, catching a glimpse of herself in the long mirror, was astonished to see that she looked almost pretty. She usually thought of herself as rather plain, but there was no doubt that tonight she looked quite striking. Probably it was the brilliant scarlet so close to her dark hair and eyes.

Their seats certainly were at the side, but they were at the front of the Stalls Circle and she knew that she would be able to see most of the great stage. It was thrilling to watch the people arriving, but quite soon she buried herself in her programme, drinking in the famous names and reading the story of *Daphnis and Chloe*, though she already knew it.

Mrs Chester sat there calmly, staring about her. Once she gave a little bow to someone in the stalls just below them, and Drina, noticing, asked: 'Who is he, Granny? Isn't he handsome?'

'Colin Amberdown, the ballet critic.'

'Oh, but – he writes books about the ballet, too. I read his *Our Changing British Ballet* not long ago.'

'Did you indeed?' said her grandmother, with a small, half-amused smile. 'Didn't you find it fairly heavy going?'

'Oh, no. Not a bit. I loved it.'

'He's heart and soul in the ballet world, and he has some connection with the Dominick School.'

It was nearly half past seven. Drina was tense with excitement as she looked round the vast place. She had once seen it on television, but she had scarcely been prepared for its hugeness.

'I am at Covent Garden!' she told herself. But she could scarcely believe it.

She still did not believe it when the music of *Les Sylphides* began and the curtain rose on the white-clad figures. How long ago it seemed since she had sat in the shabby old Grand Theatre with Mrs Pilgrim and Jenny, watching this same ballet! But she knew now that the company she had seen had indeed been third-rate, and, watching the perfection of the dancing on this far greater stage, she was filled with so great a delight that her eyelids prickled.

Her whole being seemed to follow the familiar music and it was as though she was there in spirit with those airy dancers, who had most of them left the anxious, hard years of training behind them. Though she knew, of course, that even the ballerina, at the height of her power, must still practise every day of her life.

Sitting there at Covent Garden, for the most part lost and entranced, Drina vowed at the very back of her mind that, if it was faintly possible by years of hard work, she would somehow achieve perfection. It might be impossible, of course, but she would try.

And then she forgot everything again but the ballet before her.

At the end of *Les Sylphides* Drina came very slowly back to earth and began to clap with the rest of that huge audience. The curtain rose and fell again and again and the ballerina was presented with great sheaves of flowers. She smiled and curtsied, but the audience would not let her go.

'But don't imagine yourself in that position,' said Mrs Chester, in her dry, rather tart way. 'If you do make dancing your career there'll be years of being in the corps de ballet and after that you may never be a ballerina.'

'Oh, Granny, I know,' Drina said, blinking. 'I've always known, I think. But I don't really care. Even just to be in the corps de ballet in a really good company! I think that would make me happy.'

'I hope you will be happy,' said her grandmother. 'As I've told you, it's not my idea of a good life. That's why I didn't want it for you. Now I think we'll stay here during this interval and then after *Daphnis and Chloe* we'll go up into the Crush Bar. You'll like to see the chandeliers and all the people.'

After that she did not speak again, and Drina sat there in a dream, keyed up to what was to follow. For she had still to see the greatest ballerina of the present day, who was only dancing in the main ballet. *Prima ballerina assoluta!* Of all the titles in the world that seemed to her the most satisfying.

She was very tense as the curtain went up, revealing the scene that she had seen sometimes in pictures; 'Before the Cave of the Nymphs'.

The shepherds and shepherdesses arrived to present their offerings before the nymphs of Pan and Drina stiffened to such tenseness as she watched Chloe that her back ached, though she did not realize it till afterwards. The great ballerina, as Chloe, looked so very, very young in her simple frock, and oh! the delight of her every perfect movement. It seemed to Drina as she watched that long ballet that she might never see anything so beautiful and moving again. She wanted it never to end, so that she could stay in that lovely, brilliantly coloured world, knowing such utter delight.

But the third scene ended almost before she expected it and she was left with a tear in one eye that threatened to roll down her cheek, and yet it simply mustn't, as she dared not cry over dancing before her grandmother.

The curtains, the flower-giving, the wild clapping, seemed to last for a very long time, and through it all the great dancer remained smiling and serene – almost, thought Drina, a very young girl. And yet no young girl could have that wonderful poise and assurance. All the same, it was impossible to believe that she was quite old; well over thirty.

The curtain came down for the last time and Drina felt almost worn out. It was really a good thing that her grandmother was so matter of fact.

'Yes, well, it's not a ballet that appeals to me much, but you've certainly seen some perfect dancing. Now come along quickly, or we shall never get into the Crush Bar at all.'

She bustled Drina up some stairs, along the top of a brilliantly lighted staircase and into a vast room, a-glitter with chandeliers and crowded with people, mostly in evening dress. They were thronging everywhere, all talking about the ballet and some clutching coffee cups. Drina hoped that her grandmother wouldn't insist on getting her coffee, because she was sure she would disgrace herself by dropping the cup. There was scarcely room to move.

Mrs Chester *did* insist on just that.

'I think you'd better have coffee. Stand by that pillar and I'll fetch it. Don't move, or I shall never find you again.'

'No, Granny,' Drina said meekly and she retreated obediently through the crowd to the pillar.

Mrs Chester brought two cups eventually and Drina was glad that they were in a fairly safe corner. She had drunk a little of the coffee when a male voice said close to her: 'I was hoping to get a chance to speak to you, Mrs Chester. It's many a long year since I saw you at an occasion like this!'

'Indeed it is, Mr Amberdown,' agreed Drina's

grandmother. 'I've not been near any performance of ballet since that night when *The Breton Wedding* was first danced. I've had no occasion to, and I need hardly tell you that I've been glad.'

'You never cared for the ballet,' he said. His manner was – well, it was strange, but Drina thought dazedly that he sounded respectful. Why on earth should the great Colin Amberdown be respectful to her grandmother, especially when she had just said what must be heresy to him?

Mr Amberdown's calm grey eyes looked down at Drina.

'And is this – your granddaughter? Don't tell me that you're bringing her to see ballet at last?'

'Yes, this is Andrina. And actually she brought *me*,' said Mrs Chester, with a faint chuckle. 'Marched up here by herself yesterday and came back with two tickets.'

'Hum! So it's come out, after all, has it? I know you said she should never have anything to do with the ballet.'

'I said a lot of things and meant them,' said Mrs Chester grimly. 'But it wasn't a bit of good. Drina found ballet for herself. She insisted on learning from Janetta Selswick, and now she's made me agree to letting her have an audition at one of the Schools. But we only decided two days ago, and I've made no plans yet. I suppose, though, that it will be the Dominick School.'

Drina was very shy and rather puzzled under the searching eyes. Why was he so interested in her?

'I should think it will have to be, considering that they helped to make her mother what she was. And, God knows, they'll jump at the chance of taking Ivory's daughter.'

The great chandeliers seemed to be descending on Drina in a blaze of light. The crowd seemed to her to have gone silent; the world was rocking. She heard her grandmother say: 'Take her coffee cup, for heaven's sake! She didn't know.'

'Didn't know what?' asked Colin Amberdown, taking the cup with one hand and putting the other arm behind Drina, who was grateful for the support. Things were still whirling about in the most alarming way.

'That her mother was Elizabeth Ivory. I was always afraid that she'd get hold of her life story and guess. She could hardly fail to have done. She reads so many ballet books, and I suppose there might have been something in any one of them, but –'

Things were getting back to normal, but Drina still felt hot and weak. She opened her eyes wide and stared at them.

'My mother – oh, it *can't* be true! I thought she was in the corps de ballet in some third-rate company!'

'I didn't tell her that,' said Mrs Chester hastily. 'I didn't tell her anything. But I was going to do so tomorrow.'

'Your mother,' said Mr Amberdown very clearly, 'was Elizabeth Ivory of the Igor Dominick Company. She was one of the most wonderful dancers that Britain will ever see, even greater, some think, than this

162

great dancer we have seen tonight. She died very young, of course, but even so –'

'How did she – die?' Drina asked.

'Well, she was flying to the States to appear as a guest artist with an American Company in New York and the plane crashed. You must have read that.'

'Yes, I – have. But I didn't know – I can't believe –'

'Your grandmother, who had never wanted her to be a dancer, felt that dancing led her to her death. Wasn't that so?' he asked, quite gently.

Mrs Chester said dryly: 'Yes, it was true. I always hated all that travelling that Betsy had to do. New York, Paris, Stockholm, Helsinki. Once she was famous we scarcely saw her, though she was always a loving daughter as far as she could be. Even her husband and baby scarcely saw her.'

'But she couldn't help it. Dancers have to do that,' said Drina. She had not yet really taken in the wonderful news. She still felt very wavering and odd.

'There's the bell. We'll have to go,' said Colin Amberdown. 'Well, let me know what you decide and I'll arrange it for you with the Dominick School.'

'Mr Amberdown!' cried Drina, clutching his sleeve.

'Yes?' He hesitated, looking down at her.

'Mr Amberdown, I – I haven't had time to think yet, but I know one thing *now*. Please don't tell them – don't tell *anyone* – that I'm Ivory's daughter.'

The crowd was streaming past, but he stopped dead. His eyes had lit up with quick understanding, though Mrs Chester looked startled and a trifle annoyed.

'Drina, don't be ridiculous! Why –'

'Because – because I want to be quite on my own. To work as *me*; not as Ivory's daughter. I don't want things made easy for me. I don't want people to say, "Take her because she's Ivory's daughter!" Later they can know, if I'm good, but not now. You do understand?'

'Yes, and they shan't know,' Mr Amberdown assured her. Then he patted her arm briefly and went away.

'Well, you are a strange child!' said Mrs Chester, as they made their way back to their seats. 'But you're certainly like your mother. *She* was always independent and knew her own mind. I should have thought you'd want to shout from the house-tops that Elizabeth Ivory was your mother!'

'I do! I do!' Drina cried. 'But I shan't – not yet. Oh, Granny, promise that you won't tell anyone. Not even Miss Whiteway? It's enough that *we* know!'

'I promise,' said Mrs Chester, with a very faint smile, and ushered her into her seat.

After that the last ballet was rather lost on Drina. She was still too amazed, too happy, too unbelieving. *Ivory!* Of all the great dancers of the past and present Ivory had been her mother!

She knew that she would never, as long as she lived, forget those moments under the chandeliers, when she had learned the whole truth.

Come a Stranger

by Cynthia Voigt

Mina has won a scholarship to a dance camp in Connecticut – eight whole weeks away from her family and friends, and a far cry from the close community in Crisfield she's used to. But Mina is determined to show that she can dance as well as anyone else …

From the first, Mina loved her room at camp, room 226, halfway down the long corridor. It had two beds, two windows, two dressers, two desks, and one closet which she shared with her roommate, Isadora. The beds were covered with brightly striped fabric, and the curtains matched the bedspreads. The windows looked out through the leafy branches of trees to the green quadrangle at the centre of the college. Although the room was only on the second floor, there was always a breeze to keep it comfortable, because the college had been built along the ridge of the hills that bordered the broad river.

They stayed on the campus for the whole eight weeks, except for one trip into the city of New Haven, to see a performance of *Swan Lake* at Yale University. Some of the girls, especially the older ones, complained that they felt cooped up, imprisoned, but Mina never did, not for a minute.

There were seventy people living in the dormitory, and all of them were dancers. There were four dance classes, divided by age, with sixteen girls in each class. There were three dance instructors and three assistants who were taking the master classes as well as keeping an eye on the younger students. They all lived together and ate together and worked together. Music and dance, dance and music – that was what they did, all day long. They had a dance class every morning and a music class every afternoon, taught by a professor from the college. In the evenings, there was almost always something planned, either observing one of the master classes or listening to a concert given in the small college theatre or watching a movie of a ballet or symphony. Sunday mornings they went to the non-denominational chapel, whose bells rang out over the quadrangle and dormitories to call people to worship. Mina sat amongst the dancers in an oak pew and learned a whole new set of hymns from the bound hymnals that were kept in a rack at the back of each pew with the bound prayer books. The sun shone through the stained glass windows, colouring the air with reds and greens and blues. Mina had never known how much she didn't know about dancers and about music; she looked ahead at everything she didn't know, and was glad.

There was always a song rising in her heart, one they sang at chapel on Sundays, while the collection was being taken, 'Praise God', the song rose up inside her. 'Praise God from whom all blessings flow.' Mina felt like praising God and thanking Him about all day long.

The majority of the girls had studied longer and more seriously than Mina had and knew more. Isadora, her roommate, was sure she was destined to become a famous ballerina. 'My mom says she had a feeling, even before I was born. All the time she was pregnant, she went to at least one ballet performance a week and kept music playing in the apartment. She named me after Isadora Duncan. I've got dance in my blood.'

Mina knew what it felt like to have dance in your blood. 'Who's Isadora Duncan?' she asked.

'You don't know?' Isadora looked at her, as if everybody should know, as if Mina came from a different planet.

'Nope, never heard of her. Are you going to tell me?' Mina didn't mind not knowing, she just minded not having her curiosity satisfied.

'Isadora Duncan was a great dancer, probably the greatest modern dancer. She's like Martha Graham, Twyla Tharp ...' Mina shook her head, she hadn't heard of any of these people. She tucked the names away in her memory, to learn more about them. 'Isadora Duncan was the first – she broke away from classical ballet and went back to the ancient Greeks. She wanted dance to be free from rules and things, anything artificial. She thought life shouldn't have so many rules. She danced in draperies, in bare feet, like the Greeks. Her dances were free and strong. She died young, when the scarf she was wearing got caught in the wheel of a car. See, she always wore long, long scarves around her neck.' Isadora mimed wrapping a scarf around her neck, her long arms graceful. Mina could see what Isadora Duncan must have looked like. Mina was sitting on the floor by her bed, watching Isadora. 'But her boyfriend had a convertible. The scarf got caught in the tyre and – it just snapped her neck,' Isadora concluded. 'It was a tragedy. She had lots of men, all madly in love with her, all the time.'

'What would your mother have done if you'd been a boy?'

'Named me Isadore. There are male dancers.'

Mina laughed, 'I know that.'

Charlie, short for Charlotte, who lived across the hall with Tansy, said that Isadora's mother was typical, a typical stage mother. Charlie often said things like that, in a superior way, as if she knew more. She acted closer to sixteen than eleven, most of the time. 'Typical, pushy stage mother.'

'You don't understand,' Isadora said. 'I'm going to be a prima ballerina. It's nothing to do with my mother, except she thinks I can, so she helps out. And all.'

'– and I should know,' Charlie continued, not

paying any attention. 'I've got one too. It's pretty pitiful in a way – it's because she wanted to be a singer. But she got married, instead. And had kids, instead. And keeps house, instead. And nags, nags us all.'

'Even your father?' Mina wondered.

'Especially Dad. Then she complains because Dad spends so much time out of town on business and nags him more.' Charlie shook her head, pitying the stupidity of her mother. Charlie had no intention of going on with ballet. She wanted to be in the movies. 'I'm photogenic, and – there's never the same kind of life in ballet even if you're a success, not like movies, when you're a movie actress. Ballet teaches you how to move. An actress has to know how to … move right.'

Charlie's roommate, Tansy, was a little plain girl, quiet and hard-working. Mina couldn't imagine why the camp had put Tansy and Charlie into the same room. Tansy had even been homesick for the first week, even though she really wanted to come to dance camp.

'How can you be homesick?' Mina had asked, trying to comfort her. 'Wouldn't you rather be here?'

Charlie and Isadora had exchanged a look at that. Mina caught it, out of the corner of her eyes. It was almost the kind of look kids give one another across the classroom, when they know something the teacher can't begin to understand.

'Well, I would,' Mina said to the two of them. She didn't know what they thought they knew that she didn't. 'Even though I miss my family too.'

'Your family's different,' Charlie pointed out.

'I miss my dog,' Tansy snuffled.

Mina chuckled at that, and the chuckle spread out warm into a laugh. The laugh lit up the whole dormitory room, even the farthest corners of it, and pretty soon everybody joined in, even Tansy, sitting up on the bed and blowing her nose into a tissue. She looked at Mina as if Mina was strange and wonderful.

The four of them were going to work together on the ten-minute performance that every dancer at the camp had to give for the final exercises. Their instructor, Miss Fiona Maddinton, had told them about it on the first day, after they each had an individual conference with her. In the conference, she had told each of the sixteen girls in her class what she thought when she watched them during the audition or, in Mina's case, when she looked at the tape Miss LaValle had mailed up to New York. Miss LaValle had rented a video camera up in Cambridge and Mina had performed in front of it, the *barre* exercises and a dance they had worked out to part of the *Nutcracker Suite*. 'You have strength,' Miss Maddinton said during her conference with Mina, 'and a certain rude grace. Even on that tape your presence made itself felt. A dancer has to have presence. But,' she went on, when Mina opened her mouth to ask what the teacher meant, 'you don't have discipline. It's discipline I will teach you. Natalie?' she called, indicating that the talk was over, summoning up the next girl. In the long working days, the hours of practice, Mina was learning what

170

Miss Maddinton meant. Miss Maddinton seemed pleased with her. She was surely pleased with herself: she had never worked so hard and learned so much.

The performance, Miss Maddinton had told them, could be done in groups, or individually, but had to be prepared without any adult help of any kind. Even the instructors were going to take part in the final exercises, performing for ten minutes. A lot of the girls from the class had asked Mina if she wanted to work with them, but Isadora and Charlotte and Tansy had asked her first, and she would have preferred to dance with them anyway. They were going to do an original ballet, based on Narnia. The other three had decided that, because Mina had never heard of Narnia.

'But those books have been on every reading list since I was in third grade,' Isadora said. 'Aren't they even on your summer reading list?'

'I don't have a summer reading list.'

'Then outside reading.' But Mina didn't have that either. 'You mean, you don't have to do book reports?'

'We do reports, sometimes, or projects,' Mina said, looking around at the other three. 'For science, or social studies.'

'What would I give not to have to do book reports,' Charlie sighed.

They all three lived in New York City and went to private schools, but different schools. Isadora's rich father sent plenty of money for her and her mother to live on, whether Isadora had a stepfather or not. Tansy's father was a special kind of dentist, called an orthodontist. And Charlie's father worked in advertising. Their mothers didn't have jobs and they had been interested to hear that Mina's mother did. About everything in their lives was different from Mina's, and she loved hearing them talk about their lives.

'I wouldn't mind book reports. I like reading,' Mina said.

Charlie dismissed that. 'You just don't know any better.'

'Anyway,' Isadora interrupted, 'who has an idea for what we can do?'

Tansy did. Tansy really wanted not to dance, but to choreograph. She had an idea all worked out. 'If there are two of the children, a boy and a girl – I could be the boy because I'm so small and all – and Charlie would be the girl – and Isadora would dance Aslan, all in gold, and Mina could be a Tarkaan but she'd turn into Tash, in the middle ...'

'How would she do that?' Isadora asked.

'By turning around, or maybe with a mask. I know I can think of a way,' Tansy said.

'Like in *Swan Lake*?' Mina asked. She had loved that moment when the magician swept his cape aside to reveal Odile, as if she had appeared by magic.

'Yes, or something like that. It would start out with the children on stage, being – happy or something – and then the Tarkaan would come in ...' Tansy stood up from the floor of the practice room where they were working out their project and acted out the parts. 'He'd try to be nice first and bribe them. Then he'd try to force them –'

'Force them to what?' Mina asked.

'To go with him, to be one of his people,' Isadora explained quickly. Then she said, 'I'm sorry, Mina, I didn't mean to snap at you.'

Mina hadn't been offended. She didn't think Isadora had snapped at her. She waited to hear the rest of Tansy's idea.

'Then Aslan comes in and the Tarkaan seems to give up, but he turns into Tash and they fight over the children. Aslan wins and Tash – is defeated.'

Mina could almost see the dance Tansy was talking about. 'That sounds really good,' she said. 'Doesn't it?' she asked the other two.

'What about me doing the Tarkaan, instead?' Charlie asked. 'Miss Maddinton says I'm the most dramatic dancer.'

Tansy shook her head. 'It wouldn't be as good.'

'I know what you're thinking,' Charlie argued.

'Don't be stupid,' Isadora answered. 'You're dramatic but you don't – Mina has that presence. Miss Maddinton told her that and she's right.'

'Only because I'm taller than everybody else,' Mina said, trying to pretend she wasn't flattered. It wasn't just being tall, she knew, it was her personality too.

'But can you be bad?' Tansy asked her. 'Really, really bad – Tarkaan is bad, but Tash is – evil.'

Mina stood up and turned her back to them. She thought: dark, evil, dangerous. She let that run all through her body, until she spun to face them, tall and stiff; then slowly – to music playing *lento* in her head – she went through the five positions, feet and hands, thinking all the time of dark and of evil, and how the dark, evil thing would want to spread out and wrap itself around the three girls in the room. When she finished, she smiled at them.

'Oh, wow,' Isadora said, clapping, 'that was neat. See what I mean, Charlie?'

'Yeah, I guess so.' But Charlie didn't sound convinced.

Tansy just looked at Mina, as if Mina was perfect. Mina knew she wasn't perfect, but she felt good. It was discipline that had enabled her to know exactly how to move through the positions, knowing where she wanted every muscle and every part of her body; she was learning discipline. 'I think it'll be fun,' she said.

'What music will we use?' Charlie asked.

'Something modern,' Isadora suggested.

Mina had just begun to learn about music, and she kept her mouth shut. There wasn't anything she could add to this part of the planning.

'There's some Bartok,' Tansy said. 'Piano suites, kind of simple but not really.'

'You're a walking music library,' Charlie complained.

'My mom gives me anything I want.'

They all knew that. They had all admired the stereo that was Tansy's own to bring to camp with her, and the stack of records. They all listened to Tansy's records. Mina listened more than anyone else except Tansy, because almost all of them were new to her; as if she had arrived in an unknown country with a wonderful geography, she was always ready to listen and hear something she'd never even heard of before dance camp.

'Mom says since I'm so mousy and all that, I'd better cultivate my brain –'

'Why do they all want us to get married?' Charlie cried out. 'It's not as if they were having such a good time.'

'It's crazy,' Isadora agreed.

'My mother's having a good time,' Tansy said. 'I think. She's always going out to do something interesting, getting dressed up, you know, a show or an exhibition, meeting interesting people, artists and things, having fancy dinners.'

'Who keeps your house?' Isadora asked.

'The housekeeper,' Tansy told them.

That struck them as funny.

'Mrs Welker,' Tansy said. 'Who keeps yours, Mina? When your mother's working?'

'We all do,' Mina said. 'You know, we have chores.'

'Even your father?'

'Sure.'

'Boy, if my mother tried to make my father do laundry,' Charlie said, 'or vacuum – that would be a fight that would take two weeks to blow over. We'd all starve to death in our rooms before it was safe to come down. But Dad's in advertising, and there's a lot of pressure in that. I guess your father doesn't have that kind of pressure, does he?'

Mina didn't know. 'We quarrel,' she said. Everybody quarrelled, it was human nature, and she hoped Charlie didn't feel embarrassed because her parents had fights.

Isadora's mother had been married and divorced, twice each. 'Don't I know about quarrels,' she said. 'I'd rather think about this performance.'

'I wondered,' Tansy suggested in a particularly quiet voice. Mina sat up to pay close attention. She'd learned that when Tansy used that voice, it was because what she was going to say really mattered to her. Tansy looked at Mina. 'If Mozart could work, for Aslan's music.'

'Mozart and Bartok together?' Charlie laughed.

Mina had heard some Mozart. His name often came up in the music class. She wondered if Mozart was the kind of music you could dance to, though. She didn't say anything and nobody asked her opinion. They talked on about which of Mozart's pieces they should listen to.

'I think we ought to at least try. Whatever else, Tansy really does know what she's talking about when she talks music,' Isadora finally said. 'If it works, we'll be the most original I bet.'

◉

Mina lifted her right leg on to the *barre*, toes pointed, and stretched her arms towards it. Watching herself in the mirror, she bent her neck so that it would follow perfectly the curve her back and arms made.

Then she looked back beyond herself in the mirror, seeing the whole class, all performing the same exercise, reflected back and forth in the mirrors that lined the two long walls of the room. 'Praise God', the song sang inside her, over the notes of the piano.

This was a real dance studio, as different from Miss LaValle's garage as – she didn't know anything perfect enough to compare the differences. Even though from the first minute she had stepped into it, she had felt at home, she never lost the feeling of wonder at how right the studio was. It had two narrow walls of tall windows and two long walls of mirrors that went from ceiling to floor. The upright piano filled the room with its waltz tempo for the *barre* exercises, as Miss Maddinton went up and down the line, correcting. 'That's good, Mina,' she said.

The floor was polished wood and the air was filled with light. The music went into Mina's body, and she brought her leg down in time with it, then lifted her left leg. All along the walls, mirrored back, and front, fifteen girls did the same. In the mirror, thirty-two arms stretched out. Mina let a smile spread over her face.

It was coming close to the end of camp, with only a few days left before their performance. They named their dance 'Narnia' and they were assigned to this same big studio for their rehearsals because they were a group so they needed more space. These days, the four of them came back every afternoon to rehearse. Mina could see why the instructors were making them work entirely without guidance, and she preferred it that way; but she wished she could hear what Miss Maddinton thought before the performance. Mina had been careful to listen to what Tansy said when she tried to explain how things should be danced. It wasn't that Mina was worried about their dance. She knew it was wonderful. She just thought she wanted it to be absolutely perfect. Miss Maddinton might catch something they'd missed.

Charlie called Miss Maddinton the 'White Witch', from the Narnia books, but Mina didn't see why. It wasn't as if Miss Maddinton wore only white, or had white hair, or anything like that. Her hair was dark, inky black – dyed, Charlie said – and long. She wore greys or silvery blues or silvery pinks, her leotard, tights, and wraparound skirt all the same colour. She was a professional dancer who only taught during the summer, only at this camp. Most of the year she was with a ballet company in New York.

Over the summer, Mina had written to her mother about everybody at camp, and what they were all doing. Miss Maddinton had occupied a lot of letter space, because she was a real dancer, a professional. Miss LaValle, Mina's teacher at home, had studied dance, but she was only a teacher who gave lessons in her converted garage-studio, with a record player for music. Miss LaValle was built like Miss Maddinton, both of them tall, narrow women with muscular legs, but she was older, and she wore her leotard as if it was a uniform, and it was always a plain black uniform too. Miss LaValle had taught Mina well, Mina could tell that. She liked Miss LaValle and was grateful to her. But Miss Maddinton, Miss Fiona Maddinton – she was a real ballerina. Mina wondered what Miss Maddinton would do for her own ten-minute performance, on the night. Because it got so there wasn't anything happening to write to her mother about, Mina sometimes just wrote down her guesswork about things like that: what Miss Maddinton would do, or whether Charlie's father would lose his job because he had lost a big account. Her mother wrote back the news from home, that Zandor got a fifty-cent-an-hour raise and had a new girlfriend, that Belle was bored (and boring, Mina's mother added), messages from Mina's father and from Louis, and her own opinions about the summer minister's sermons and his family. It sounded like Mina's mother liked the minister fine, but wasn't sure about his wife. 'We don't see much of her,' Momma wrote.

Mina had started off writing to Kat, just silly things and Kat had written back, but after a couple of weeks that had tapered off. Kat couldn't possibly understand how wonderful it was. Mina couldn't have explained, for instance, how much she liked learning about music, its history, the names of composers, and listening to their different music, the different forms music could be written in. Mr Tattodine, who liked Mina because she asked so many questions, had white hair that flopped over his

179

forehead, and a way – when the class was listening to a record – of getting entirely engrossed in the music, until his face looked half asleep and his hand would come up to mark the beat, as if he was conducting the piece.

It was Mr Tattodine who had given Tansy the idea for where to find the right Mozart music for Aslan. Tansy had been trying movements from symphonies and string quartets, but nothing worked. Nothing made a dance. During the classes on opera, when he was talking about Mozart's life and the reasons that people thought he was a genius, Mr Tattodine had mentioned *The Magic Flute*. 'It was considered at the time that he had written a low piece of work, a popular effort, written for money. Well, he did need money, he always needed money. But it is now taken as one of his richest works, musically speaking,' Mr Tattodine said. Then he smiled at them and said, 'I'm sorry, I'm lecturing at you again, I keep forgetting. Let's have a question. Who can define the differences between opera and ballet? The musical differences, that is, because many operas – like *The Magic Flute* – do include dance.' Tansy nudged Mina then.

Mina knew four of the seven differences that were given and realized once again how glad she was to be at camp. Mr Tattodine said the way she learned was like a sponge or a vacuum cleaner; 'But not in the bad sense,' he said. Mina wasn't worried about bad or good senses; she knew she could remember almost everything she was told, and she learned that she could hear not only musical phrases and forms, not only harmony and counterpoint, but also the several individual instruments that played together. She loved the whole range of strings, the variety of percussions, the winds and the reeds. Mr Tattodine had them try playing every instrument, just to get the sound out of it. Mina's favourites were the reeds, because to play them you needed to hold the reed properly, which took discipline; but it was also a matter of your breath going through the wooden tube. The reeds seemed the most complicated and natural.

The brasses were her next favourite. When she had the French horn in her hands, in class, she got a clear note out of it, without any trouble, a round winding sound that made you sit up at attention and called out to you. 'I've just got a lot of hot air,' Mina said laughing and passed the horn to Isadora. 'That's why I'm not having any trouble with it.'

Once Tansy had listened to *The Magic Flute* and found passages of music that she wanted in it, passages that would be like counterpoint to Tarkaan's Bartok, they moved ahead with their dance. It took work, hours of practising to get the steps right, to get each individual performance right, to get everything put together right so that the dance worked the way Tansy wanted it to. But hours of work were no trouble. Charlie and Isadora complained, sometimes, but Mina never even felt like it.

'What are you, some goody-goody?' Charlie demanded during their second-to-last rehearsal.

'It's because her daddy's a minister,' Isadora, stretched out on the floor beside Charlie, said. Tansy had been called out to the phone, which was odd because parents usually called during the hour the girls had free before lights out. Mina was trying to get Charlie to go over the part where Tarkaan was trying to win over the human girl. Charlie didn't see the point of doing it without having Tansy there to watch, because they'd just have to do it all over again for Tansy.

'I think she's just stronger than we are,' Charlie said. 'You don't get as tired, Mina; you can't argue that.'

Mina didn't know what it was, except that she liked what she was doing so much that she never got tired doing it. She decided to listen to the Bartok again.

Mr Tattodine had explained to her the way the rhythm worked and the reasons for the notes being what they were and the different scale Bartok was using. She didn't really understand, but she could hear the dance in the music now. Mr Tattodine was an immigrant, from Hungary, which was Bartok's homeland. He said maybe that was why the music made sense to him. Mina listened to the fragmented chords of the Bartok, standing still but feeling as if her body was moving to the dance.

Tansy came back through the big door at the end of the room. 'Everything OK?' Isadora asked.

'My grandfather died.'

'Oh. That's too bad,' Isadora said.

'Were you close?' Charlie asked.

Tansy shook her head. 'I've barely seen him since he went into the nursing home.'

'Was he sick?' Mina asked.

'Maybe we ought to stop the rehearsal,' Charlie suggested.

'The performance is the day after tomorrow,' Tansy said. 'We don't have enough time as it is. I'm sort of sad, but it's not as if … He wasn't sick, he just got too old to take care of himself, so he went into a home.'

Charlie and Isadora started telling stories about old relatives of their parents who had gone into nursing homes, or retired to places where there were a lot of old people gathered together. Mina didn't say anything, because her one set of living grandparents lived with her mother's brother in Georgia, and the grandparents who had died when she was still a baby had lived just around the corner. She thought of Miz Hunter, but didn't mention her either. After a while, Tansy said it was time to get back to work, 'If that's OK?'

They were the last of the youngest class to give their performance. By the time they moved on stage, Mina had been so nervous for so long she was too tired to be tense. Mr Tattodine played the tape they had put together. Mina listened to the first bars of music and watched the curtain draw apart. She wore her black leotard and a mask over her eyes, a black Halloween mask that she had edged with red and gold glitter; Isadora, with her long hair loose, like

183

Aslan's golden mane, wore a golden leotard and tights; Charlie wore white, with a skirt wrapped around it, and Tansy wore green. The other three had to buy new leotards, but Mina just had to buy the mask, which was lucky. Tansy had thought everything out. Mina's part required angular steps and positions, while Isadora, as Aslan, moved in arcs and circles. Isadora never came into Mina's part of the stage, until the end; Mina sometimes moved a little into Isadora's part, like the tip of a triangle, but she danced out quickly. The two children in Narnia went back and forth.

When Mina changed into Tash himself, all she did was take the mask off. They had painted her eyebrows dark and her mouth red and larger than it was. The music's sharp lines of melody, broken off, matched her steps. As Tansy had explained it to them, Tash made triangles and Aslan circles. All the dancing showed that, just as the music clashed and couldn't ever be made to play together. So Isadora moved in circles, leaping, turning, golden, while Mina moved dark and strong and cruel to the points of triangles. At the end, Aslan's circles wound all around Tash, and he was driven from the stage. Then the two children and Aslan danced together, to Mozart.

When they took their bows at the end, everybody in the audience stood up to clap. They held hands and bowed and bowed, still breathing heavily, smiling at one another and at the audience. At the reception afterwards, punch and cookies served in

the dormitory living room, just about everybody in the camp came up to tell Mina what a good job she'd done.

'Thanks.' She smiled. She couldn't stop smiling. She wished – that they hadn't performed yet and that it was something she could do again, right away.

Miss Maddinton came up, with another instructor, while Mina was getting another cup of punch. 'It was very good, Mina,' Miss Maddinton said. 'You've learned a lot this summer, haven't you?'

'Yes.' Mina knew she had.

'I envy you that class, Fiona,' the other instructor said. 'And you, young lady, you were absolutely frightening. I was on the edge of my chair.'

'It's Tansy, really,' Mina said. 'It was her dance, her idea, and all.'

'You don't have to be so modest,' Miss Maddinton corrected her.

Mina smiled. She felt goofy smiling so much, but she couldn't stop. 'Thank you. But it really was Tansy.'

'I know that; do you think I don't know that?' Miss Maddinton said.

Mr Tattodine came up to the four of them. 'You've had the success of the evening, and I'm very proud of you. It was good theatre,' he said to Tansy.

Tansy lowered her head, embarrassed and pleased. Mina smiled.

'And well danced all of you. You have shown me that ballet is still a living art. Oh, I've enjoyed your performance.'

They all had trouble going to sleep that night. They all sat around in Mina's room, in the dark, talking in low voices. It was the last night of camp, and Mina suddenly felt as if she couldn't bear to wait the whole school year before she came back.

'It's not that we were the best,' Tansy was saying, trying to put their feelings into words.

'Except that we were awfully good for our age,' Isadora said.

'I hate that for-your-age stuff, don't you?' Charlie protested.

'We were the only really original ones,' Mina said. 'Everybody else, except the instructor for the oldest class, danced the usual dances and even hers – she danced to jazz but it was still traditional. Ours wasn't like anybody else's.' She smiled.

'It was worth all that work, Tansy, I'll admit it,' Charlie said.

'Yeah, thanks,' Isadora agreed. 'And to Mina too – did you hear the way somebody gasped when you took off your mask, Mina? I don't know what they expected to see. It was like a horror show.'

Mina smiled. 'Thanks a lot,' she joked.

'You know what I mean.'

'I'm already wondering what Tansy's going to ask us to do next year, aren't you?' Mina asked them. She had got so much better in just the weeks here. She could work every day, practically, if she got organized, and by next summer – 'Oh, I'm looking forward to next summer,' she said.

'Mina! We've still got two weeks of vacation. What's wrong with you?' Charlie demanded. 'Don't wish away my only vacation time.'

Mina thought that camp was her vacation, but she didn't say so. They heard the college bell chime two in the morning before they finally were sleepy enough to go to bed.

◎

Miss Maddinton was the one who greeted Mina's father when he drove up. She made her report as he loaded Mina's suitcase into the back seat of the dusty car. 'She's learned a lot about discipline this summer.'

All around them, girls were greeting their families, saying goodbye to their friends, getting into cars, driving away. Mina waved and waved to Tansy, going off in a red sports car with her father, who looked as small and mousy as Tansy.

'I've enjoyed having her in class. It seems to have been a good experience for everybody.'

'I know she's had a good time here,' Mina's father said. 'We thank you.'

'See you next summer, Mina,' Miss Maddinton answered. 'Keep practising.'

'Oh I will,' Mina promised.

She got into the car. Her father got into the car. She turned her head to look at him. 'You better belt in,' he said. Then he reached out a big arm to hug her, and she hugged him back. There hadn't been any hugging or hand-holding or putting arms around all summer long. Mina thought, for a minute, that she thought there should have been, but then she dismissed the idea. It wouldn't have been right for a dance camp; it wouldn't have suited.

'We've got a long drive ahead,' her father said. He drove down the road beside the river, then along the ramp and out into the speeding traffic. He didn't talk. Her father didn't like these crowded throughways, Mina remembered. He was concentrating hard. She didn't like them much either, once it stopped being exciting to be hurtling along, rushing, once the sad feelings started coming up again inside her, at leaving and having to be gone from camp for so long. The truck motors roared in her ears, the hot air smelled of gasoline and oil, and the scenery at the roadside was mostly the backs of houses, backs of shopping centres, backs of factories. Mina sat quiet, remembering, feeling sad.

'Mina?' her father asked.

Mina turned her head to look at him. She had forgotten how rich the sound of his voice was.

'Were you the only little black girl there at camp?'

'I guess so,' Mina said.

'Why was that?'

'I was the only one good enough, I guess,' Mina said.

The Mysterious
Miss Minning

by Harriet Castor

Crumblewood College was not like other schools. It was not even like other ballet schools (which, let's face it, are a curious set of places at the best of times).

From the outside, it looked like a large, rather saggy old house, the kind that a Duke or Duchess might once have lived in. The drive was a whole mile long, and when you got to the end of it, you found yourself at a massive wooden front door, with rows of windows stretching off on either side, and a square tower looming above.

On this particular day, the tower was bathed in rosy morning sunshine. The flag on the flagpole at the tower's top was fluttering in a warm breeze, showing the Crumblewood College crest – crossed tutus with Swan Queens rampant – to anyone who cared to look.

No one did care to look. The birds were too busy tumbling about in the trees, and everyone else was in Assembly.

'... which pains me greatly,' the headteacher, Mrs

Lavington, was saying, 'because running in the corridors is such a totally *unnecessary* and *foolish* activity, leading all too often to *injury*.'

In some ways, Crumblewood College was just like other schools.

In the third row from the back, Melanie Gristwood whispered out of the corner of her mouth, 'Are you telling me she's a normal woman? Seriously? Look at those eyes – look at that hair! She's spooky all over ...'

It wasn't Mrs Lavington she was talking about. No one could call Mrs Lavington – all egg-stained cardigan and sensible lace-ups – *spooky*. No, the person Mel was referring to was sitting behind Mrs Lavington, partly in shadow, straight-backed and inscrutable as a Zen master.

The black clothes seemed to melt into one another. The sleek hair – darker than a moonless midnight sky – was scraped back into a tight knot. Beneath it a pale disc floated in the dim light: a face, with eyes curiously pale, like a cat's. Curiously pale and curiously bright.

Beside Mel, her best friend Alice Thonkleton whispered back, 'OK, so if she's a weirdy with spooky powers, how come she can't hear us talking about her?'

At that exact moment Miss Minning – deputy head, and subject of this speculation – chose to turn and look directly at Mel and Alice.

Mel jumped. The hairs on the back of her neck prickled to attention. She heard Alice gulp. Neither of them said another word.

'And now for some jollier news,' said Mrs Lavington, shuffling her papers. 'I am proud and privileged to announce that Erik Zveginzov will be the outside examiner for our Assessments this year.'

There was a muffled groan. No one had anything against Erik Zveginzov. It was just that Assessments were the most dreaded event in the school calendar.

'As you all know,' Mrs Lavington went on, 'Mr Zveginzov is an international star with a fearsomely busy schedule. It was quite a task to persuade him to come at all, and for that we have to thank Miss Minning and her almost, one might say, *magical* powers of persuasion.'

Mel's fingers sought the nearest bit of Alice, and gave her a significant pinch.

In the changing room after Assembly, as Mel and Alice were getting dressed for ballet along with the rest of their class, the air was thick with talk of the Assessments. The awful thing about them was that, every year, the pupils who didn't pass were asked to leave.

'More people will get the boot this time,' said the girl next to Mel, a collection of hairgrips clamped between her teeth. 'A fifth former told me ours is the year they really sort the Darceys from the dodos. 'Cos in September the best ones'll go into Minning's class, and they don't want too many stragglers.'

'The sooner they cut out the dead wood the better, in my opinion,' drawled another voice. This was Tabitha Fanthorpe, self-proclaimed owner of the Best Feet in the Class (and Possibly the World). Tabitha found ballet *easy* (she said), and was – Mel had to admit – infuriatingly good at it.

Standing at the *barre* a few minutes later while their

teacher marked out a *plié* exercise, Mel found herself feeling hot and cold all over. She had wanted to get into Miss Minning's class ever since her first week at Crumblewood, when she had seen Miss Minning floating (she was sure of it) down the corridor.

True, it was a frightening prospect. But people went into Miss Minning's class hardly able to turn a single *pirouette*, and came out sailing round three or four times, easy breezy.

There were rumours that she taught you how to jump and *not come down*.

There were rumours that you learnt not just how to balance on one leg – but on *no* legs, too.

There were also rumours that for the first six months Miss Minning made you sit facing a wall, learning concentration.

The most curious thing of all, though, was that once somebody joined Miss Minning's class, you could never get them to talk about it, however much of a chatterbox they'd been beforehand.

And Mel was a sucker for a mystery. What went on in Miss Minning's classes? She just had to know. Which meant she just had to pass this Assessment.

◉

That night after lights out, Mel and Alice crept to the window of the bedroom they shared and hauled up the sash. With a rumble, they heard their friends in the room next door, Fran and Trudi, doing the same. They always said good night this way.

'By the way, I heard Mrs Lavington talking to that Zveginzov bloke on the phone,' whispered Fran, as loudly as she dared. 'Our Assessment's fixed for the day after tomorrow.'

'So soon!' wailed Alice.

Mel didn't say a word. She turned back into the room to look at herself in the mirror. And sighed.

The thing was, Mel wasn't what you'd call natural ballerina material. She wasn't petite like Alice, or willowy like Fran. She had big hands and feet. She had knees that were verging on the knobbly. Even her hair wouldn't behave – it sprung from her head in tight little curls, and was about as sleek as a sheep's woolly jumper. But she loved dancing more than anything else in the world. If she had to give it up … it would feel like giving up breathing.

'What if it's me this year?' Mel whispered a few minutes later, when Alice had shut the window and they were climbing into bed. ' "Melanie Gristwood, you are the weakest link – goodbye!" I mean, look at me. Hands like wet halibut, gangly as a drunk giraffe. *I*'d throw me out!'

'No, no,' insisted Alice. 'I'd throw *me* out.'

'You? Ha!' said Mel. 'Take a look at yourself, Alice. You've got flat turn out, you can get your legs round your earholes, and your natural style of movement is *wafting*.'

Alice frowned. 'Thanks very much.'

'You're welcome,' said Mel. And she yanked the duvet up to her chin.

◉

Thwunk! The studio door swung open. Miss Minning and Erik Zveginzov entered, gliding and striding

195

respectively. At the *barre*, a line of pupils standing in first position pulled up their knees even tighter, tucked their bottoms under and tried, largely unsuccessfully, not to look nervous.

Miss Minning and Mr Zveginzov installed themselves in chairs. Miss Minning had a clipboard. Mr Zveginzov had muscles that Mel found quite mesmerizing.

'Prepare: one-and-a two-and-a three ...' intoned the class teacher, Miss Everett, and Mel snapped her attention back to the exercise. As she lifted her arm into first position, she noticed her fingers trembling.

Be brilliant, be *brilliant* ... Mel urged herself silently, over and over. But she found that the harder she tried, the more seemed to go wrong. She wobbled in *fondus*, and when it came to *frappés* her brain turned to spaghetti – she just couldn't get the exercise right.

It didn't help that Tabitha Fanthorpe was standing directly behind her, and spent the whole of *grands battements* kicking Mel up the bottom.

'Oi!' hissed Mel. 'Cut it out, will you?'

'This class is too crowded,' Tabitha hissed back. 'The sooner you go, Gristwood, the better.'

◎

'It was awful! A total, utter disaster!'

'It wasn't that bad.'

'Did you see my *adage*? I *fell over*.'

'Everyone knows there's a wonky floorboard in that corner.'

'It wasn't a wonky floorboard. It was a wonky me.'

Mel and Alice were in the dinner queue, shuffling

slowly past framed photographs of Crumblewood's illustrious ex-pupils. Mel could hardly bear to look at all those proud Prince Siegfrieds and smiling Lilac Fairies.

'I can't believe they don't tell us the results for a fortnight,' groaned Mel. 'It's cruel. It's torture.'

'Are you going to moan all the time?' asked Alice. 'For two whole weeks?'

'Definitely,' said Mel.

'Then it *is* torture,' said Alice.

'You know what, Mel?' said Alice ten minutes later, when they were sitting with their trays. 'I think you should take matters into your own hands.'

'What d'you mean?'

Alice's normally serious little face was bright with excitement. She leaned forward. 'I dare you to go into Miss Minning's rooms and see if you can find your Assessment report.'

'You ... you wouldn't!' Mel was shocked.

'I just did.'

Dares were serious things. Mel and Alice awarded points for them, and kept a running score. Refusal meant points deducted.

Mel gulped. 'But ... what if she caught me?'

Alice smiled sweetly. 'If you really think you're going to get chucked out, what do you have to lose?'

That night, Crumblewood College sat hunched like a giant stone toad in the inky darkness. Only the dimmest of night-lights glowed in its corridors. Somewhere, an owl hooted and behind closed bedroom doors, two hundred pupils stirred and turned over in their sleep.

The two-hundred-and-first, one Melanie Gristwood, stopped in her tracks, her bare feet chilly on the cold lino floor. Inside her chest, her heart was pounding like it wanted to get out.

She had reached the bottom of a stone spiral staircase. Above her lay the tower rooms where Miss Minning lived. Taking one deep, shuddering breath and angling her torch-beam down on to the steps, Mel began to climb.

The staircase made three whole revolutions before a door appeared. It was wooden, and pointed at the top liked a church window. It was also ajar.

The slice of room Mel could see through the crack showed her the edge of a desk, piled neatly with books. 'Study,' said Mel to herself with relief (she had feared coming upon Miss Minning in her bed). There was no light on. Since the idea of Miss Minning sitting there in the dark was just too scary, Mel decided that the room was empty. Gingerly, she pushed the door further open and stole inside.

Assessment reports – where would they be? Mel shone her torch on the desktop, and noticed that in amongst the books there was a single stack of paper. The top sheet had a little writing on it – just a line or two. Stealthily, Mel approached, and bent to read it.

'Melanie Gristwood –' she read. 'A remarkable, unusual talent. Would improve vastly if she had more confidence. My class.'

The words floated before Mel's eyes. A warm feeling spread through her, like runny honey trickling deliciously down her insides.

That was all the paper said. Mel didn't dare disturb it to see what was written on the sheets underneath. It was only later that it struck Mel as an astonishing coincidence that her report, and her report alone should be lying there in full view. Almost ... but what a silly thought! Almost as if she had been expected.

Now, though, with nothing more on her mind than relief that she had not been seen, Mel tiptoed back down the staircase. As she did so, a slender figure in a

silk kimono dressing gown leaned out of the doorway to watch her go. Then, with a secret smile, Miss Minning turned back into her room, and softly closed the door.

Mel gazed out at the warm September sunshine and smiled. It was funny how things had turned out last term. Who would've predicted that Tabitha Fanthorpe would fail her Assessment? 'The word on the corridors,' Alice had whispered at the time, 'is that Minning reckons Tab's smug and lazy. And no amount of talent makes up for *that*.'

Alice herself had survived to start this new term (phew!), and Fran and Trudi too. What Mel had found utterly mind-wobblingly amazing, though, was that of the four of them only she had been asked to join Miss Minning's class.

It was little wonder that for the past few nights she'd barely had a wink's sleep. Now Mel swallowed hard, turned away from the window and checked the corridor clock for the fifth time. Ten to three. Class was about to begin.

Her heart had started a crazy excited jig, and it felt as though her stomach was trying to turn itself inside out. This was the moment she'd been waiting for. Miss Minning's secrets were about to be revealed. Mel took a deep breath. 'Unusual talent,' she recited to herself. 'Would improve vastly if she had more confidence.'

Then, stretching out a hand, Mel pushed on the studio door and stepped inside.

The Rose of
Puddle Fratrum

by Joan Aiken

Right, then: imagine this little village, not far back from the sea, in the chalk country. Puddle Fratrum is its name. One dusty, narrow street, winding along from the Haymakers' Arms to Mrs Sherborne's Bed and Breakfast (with french marigolds and bachelors' buttons in the front garden): halfway between these two, at an acute bend, an old old, grey stone house, right on the pavement, but with a garden behind hidden from the prying eyes of strangers by a high wall. And the house itself – now here's a queer thing – the house itself covered all over *thick*, doors, windows, and all, by a great climbing rose, fingering its way up to the gutters and over the stone-slabbed roof, sending out tendrils this way and that, round corners, over sills, through crevices, till the place looks not so much like a house, more like a mound of vegetation, a great green thorny thicket.

In front of it, a BBC man, standing and scratching his head.

Presently the BBC man, whose name was Rodney Cushing, walked along to the next building, which was a forge.

TOBIAS PROUT, BLACKSMITH AND FARRIER, said the sign, and there he was, white-haired, leather-aproned, with a pony's bent knee gripped under his elbow, trying on a red-hot shoe for size.

Rodney waited until the fizzling and sizzling and smell of burnt coconut had died down, and then he asked, 'Can you tell me if that was the ballerina's house?' – pointing at the rose-covered clump.

BBC men are used to anything, but Rodney was a bit startled when the blacksmith, never even answering, hurled the red-hot pony shoe at the stone wall of his forge (where it buckled into a figure-eight and sizzled some more), turned his back, and stomped to an inner room where he began angrily working his bellows and blowing up his forge fire.

Rodney, seeing no good was to be had from the blacksmith, walked along to the Haymakers' Arms.

'Can you tell me,' he said to Mr Donn the land-lord over a pint of old and mild, 'can you tell me anything about the house with the rose growing over it?'

'Arr,' said the landlord.

'Did it belong to a ballet dancer?'

'Maybe so.'

'Famous thirty years back?'

'Arr.'

'By name Rose Collard?'

'Arr,' said the landlord. 'The Rose of Puddle

Fratrum, they did use to call her. And known as far afield as Axminster and Poole.'

'She was known all over the world.'

'That may be. I can only speak for these parts.'

'I'm trying to make a film about her life, for the BBC. I daresay plenty of people in the village remember her?'

'Arr. Maybe.'

'I was asking the blacksmith, but he didn't answer.'

'Deaf. Deaf as an adder.'

'He didn't seem deaf,' Rodney said doubtfully.

'None so deaf as them what won't hear. All he hears is nightingales.'

'Oh. How very curious. Which reminds me, can you put me up for the night?'

'Not I,' said the landlord gladly. 'Old Mrs Sherborne's fule enough for that, though; she'll have ye.'

Mrs Sherborne, wrinkled and tart as a dried apricot, was slightly more prepared to be communicative about the Rose of Puddle Fratrum.

'My second cousin by marriage, poor thing,' she said, clapping down a plate with a meagre slice of Spam, two lettuce leaves, and half a tomato. 'Slipped on a banana-peel, she did ('twas said one of the scene-shifters dropped it on the stage); mortification set in, they had to take her leg off, that was the end of her career.'

'Did she die? Did she retire? What happened to her?'

In his excitement and interest, Rodney swallowed Spam, lettuce, tomato, and all, at one gulp. Mrs Sherborne pressed her lips together and carried away his plate.

'Came back home, went into a decline, never smiled again,' she said, returning with two prunes and half a dollop of junket so thickly powdered over with nutmeg that it looked like sandstone. 'Let the rose grow all over the front of her house, wouldn't answer the door, wouldn't see a soul. Some say she died. Some say she went abroad. Some say she's still there and the nightingales fetch her food. (Wonderful lot of nightingales we do have hereabouts, all the year round.) But one thing they're all agreed on.'

'What's that?' The prunes and junket had gone the way of the Spam in one mouthful; shaking her head, Mrs Sherborne replaced them with two dry biscuits and a square centimetre of processed cheese wrapped in a seamless piece of foil that defied all attempts to discover its opening.

'When she hurt her leg she was a-dancing in a ballet that was writ for her special. About a rose and a nightingale, it was. They say that for one scene they had to have the stage knee-deep in rose-petals – fresh every night, too! Dear, dear! Think of the cost!'

Mrs Sherborne looked sadly at the mangled remains of the cheese (Rodney had managed to haggle his way through the foil somehow) and carried it away.

'Well, and so?' Rodney asked, when she came back into the dark, damp little parlour with a small cup of warm water into which a minute quantity of Dark Tan shoe-polish had almost certainly been dissolved. 'What about this ballet?'

''Twas under all the rose-petals the banana-peel had been dropped. That was how she came to slip on it. So when Rose Collard retired she laid a curse on the ballet – she came of a witch family, there's always been a-plenty witches in these parts, as well as nightingales,' Mrs Sherborne said, nodding dourly, and Rodney thought she might easily qualify for membership of the Puddle Fratrum and District Witches' Institute herself – 'laid a curse on the ballet. "Let no company ever put it on again," says she, a-sitting in her wheelchair, "or, sure as I sit here –"'

'Sure as I sit here, what?' asked Rodney eagerly.

'I disremember exactly. The dancer as took Rose's part would break *her* leg, or the stage'd collapse, or there'd be some other desprat mischance. Anyway, from that day to this, no one's ever dared to do that ballet, not nowhere in the world.'

Rodney nodded gloomily. He already knew this. It had been extremely difficult even to get hold of a copy of the score and choreographic script. *The Nightingale and the Rose* had been based on a version of a story by Oscar Wilde. Music had been specially written by Augustus Irish, choreography by Danny Pashkinski, costumes and scenery designed by Rory el Moro. The original costumes were still laid away in mothballs in the Royal Museum of Ballet. Rodney was having nylon copies made for his film.

'Well, you won't be wanting nothing *more*, I don't

suppose,' Mrs Sherborne said, as if Rod might be expected to demand steak tartare and praline ice. 'Here's the bath plug. I dare say you will wish to retire as the TV's out of order. Put the plug back in the kitchen after you've had your bath.'

This was presumably to discourage Rodney from the sin of taking two baths in quick succession, but he had no wish to do so. The water was hardly warmer than the coffee. When he ran it into the tiny bath, a sideways trickle from the base of the tap flowed on to the floor, alarming an enormous spider so much that all the time Rodney was in the bath he could hear it scurrying agitatedly about the linoleum. A notice beside a huge canister of scouring powder said PLEASE LEAVE THIS BATH CLEAN, after which some guest with spirit still unbroken had added WHY USE IT OTHERWISE?

Shivering, Rodney dropped the bath plug in the kitchen sink and went to his room. But the bed had only one thin, damp blanket; he got dressed again, and leaned out of the window. Some nightingales were beginning to tune up in the distance. The summer night was cool and misty, with a great vague moon sailing over the dim silvered roofs of Puddle Fratrum. Due to the extreme curve in the village street, the corner of Mrs Sherborne's back garden touched on another, enclosed by a high wall, which Rod was almost sure was that of the legendary Rose Collard.

He began to ponder. He scratched his head.

Then, going to his suitcase, he extracted a smallish piece of machinery, unfolded it, and set it up.

It stood on one leg, with a tripod foot.

Rodney pulled out a kind of drawer on one side of this gadget, revealing a bank of lettered keys. On these he typed the message, 'Hello, Fred.'

The machine clicked, rumbled, let out one or two long experimental rasping chirrs, not at all unlike the nightingales warming up, and then replied in a loud creaking voice, 'Friday evening June twelve nineteen-seventy, eight-thirty p.m. Good evening, Rodney.'

The door shot open. Mrs Sherborne came boiling in.

'What's this?' she cried indignantly. 'I let the room to *one*, no more. Entertaining visitors in bedrooms is strictly against the –' She stopped, her mouth open. 'What's that?'

'My travelling computer,' Rodney replied.

Mrs Sherborne gave the computer a long, doubtful, suspicious glare. But at last she retired, saying, 'Well, all right. But if there's any noise, or bangs, mind, or if neighbours complain, you'll have to leave, immediate!'

'I have problems, Fred,' Rodney typed rapidly as soon as the door closed. 'Data up to the present about Rose Collard are as follows': and he added a summary of all that he had learned, adding, 'People in the village are unhelpful. What do you advise?'

Fred brooded, digesting the information that had been fed in. 'You should climb over the garden wall,' he said at length.

'I was afraid you'd suggest that,' Rodney typed resignedly. Then he closed Fred's drawer and folded his leg, took a length of rope from a small canvas holdall, and went downstairs. Mrs Sherborne poked her head out of the kitchen when she heard Rodney open the front door.

'I lock up at ten sharp,' she snapped.

'I hope you have fun,' Rodney said amiably, and went out.

He walked a short way, found a narrow alley to his left, and turned down it, finding, as he had hoped, that it circled round behind the walled garden of the rose-covered house. The wall, too, was covered by a climbing rose, very prickly, and although there was a door at the back it was locked, and plainly had not been opened for many years.

Rodney tossed up one end of his rope, which had a grappling-hook attached, and flicked it about until it gripped fast among the gnarled knuckles of the roses.

Inside the wall half a dozen nightingales were singing at the tops of their voices.

'The place sounds like a clock factory,' Rodney thought, pulling himself up and getting badly scratched. Squatting on top of the wall, he noticed that all the nightingales had fallen silent. He presumed that they were staring at him but he could not see them; the garden was full of rose-bushes run riot into massive clumps; no doubt the nightingales were sitting in these. But between the rose thickets were stretches of silvery grass; first freeing and winding up his rope, Rodney jumped down and began to wander quietly about. The nightingales started tuning up once more.

Rodney had not gone very far when something

tapped him on the shoulder.

He almost fell over, so quickly did he spin round.

He had heard nothing, but there was a person behind him, sitting in a wheelchair. Uncommon sight she was, to be sure, the whole of her bundled up in a shawl, with a great bush of moon-silvered white hair (he could see the drops of mist on it) and a long thin black stick (which was what she had tapped him with), ash-white face, thinner than the prow of a Viking ship, and a pair of eyes as dark as holes, steadily regarding him.

'And what do *you* want?' she said coldly.

'I – I'm sorry, miss – ma'am,' Rodney stammered. 'I did knock, but nobody answered the door. Are you – could you be – Miss Rose Collard?'

'If I am,' said she, 'I don't see *that's* a cause for any ex-Boy Scout with a rope and an extra share of impertinence to come climbing into my garden.'

'I'm from the BBC. I – we did write – care of Covent Garden. The letter was returned.'

'Well? I never answer letters. Now you *are* here, what do you want?'

'We are making a film about your life. Childhood in Puddle Fratrum. Career. And scenes from the ballet that was written for you.'

'So?'

'Well, Miss Collard, it's this curse you laid on it. I –' He hesitated, jabbed his foot into a dew-sodden silvery tussock of grass, and at last said persuasively, 'I don't suppose you could see your way to take the curse *off* again?'

'Why?' she asked with interest. 'Is it working?'

'*Working!* We've had one electrician's strike, two musicians', three studio fires, two cameras exploded, five dancers sprained their ankles. It's getting to be almost impossible to find anyone to take the part now.'

'My part? Who have you got at present?'

'A young dancer called Tessa Porutska. She's pretty inexperienced but – well, no one else would volunteer.'

Rose Collard smiled.

'So – well – couldn't you take the curse off? It's

such a long time since it all happened.'

'Why should I take it off? What do I care about your studio fires or your sprained ankles?'

'If I brought Tess to see you? She's so keen to dance the part.'

'So was I keen once,' Rose Collard said, and she quoted dreamily, ' "One red rose is all I want," cried the Nightingale.'

'It's such a beautiful ballet,' pleaded Rodney, 'or at least it *would* be, if only the stage didn't keep collapsing, and the props going astray, and the clarinettist getting hiccups –'

'Really? Did all those things happen? I never thought it would work half so well,' Rose Collard said wistfully, as if she rather hoped he would ask her to a rehearsal.

'What exactly were the terms of the curse?'

'Oh, just that some doom or misfortune should prevent the ballet ever being performed right through till Puddle church clock ran backwards, and the man who dropped the banana-peel said he was sorry, and somebody put on the ballet with a company of one-legged dancers.'

Rodney, who had looked moderately hopeful at the beginning of this sentence, let out a yelp of despair.

'We could probably fix the church clock. And surely we could get the chap to say he was sorry – where is he now, by the way?'

'How should I know?'

'But *one-legged* dancers! Have a heart, Miss Collard!'

'*I've* only got one leg!' she snapped. 'And I get along. Anyway it's not so simple to take off a curse.'

'But wouldn't you like to?' he urged her. 'Wouldn't you enjoy seeing the ballet? Doesn't it get a bit boring, sitting in this garden year after year, listening to all those jabbering nightingales?'

There was an indignant silence for a moment, then a chorus of loud, rude jug-jugs.

'Well –' she said at last, looking half convinced, 'I'll think about it. Won't promise anything. At least – I tell you what, I'll make a bargain. You fix about the church clock and the apology, I'll see what I can do about remitting the last bit of the curse.'

'Miss Collard,' said Rodney, 'you're a prime gun!' and he was so pleased that he gave her a hug. The wheelchair shot backwards, Miss Collard looked very much surprised, and the nightingales all exclaimed,

'Phyooo – jug-jug-jug, tereu, tereu!'

Rodney climbed back over the wall with the aid of his rope. Mrs Sherborne had locked him out, so he spent the night more comfortably than he would have in her guest room, curled up on a bed of hassocks in the church. The clock woke him by striking every quarter, so he rose at 6.45 and spent an hour and a half tinkering with the works, which hung down like a sporran inside the bell tower and could be reached by means of his rope.

'No breakfasts served after 8.15!' snapped Mrs Sherborne, when Rodney appeared in her chilly parlour. Outside the windows mist lay thick as old-man's-beard.

'It's only quarter to,' he pointed out mildly. 'Hark!'

'That's funny,' she said, listening to the church clock chime. 'Has that thing gone bewitched, or have I?'

Rodney sat down quietly and ate his dollop of cold porridge, bantam's egg, shred of marmalade and thimbleful of tea. Then he went off to the public callbox to telephone his fiancée Miss Tessa Prout (Porutska for professional purposes) who was staying at the White Lion Hotel in Bridport along with some other dancers and a camera team.

'Things aren't going too badly, love,' he told her. 'I think it might be worth your while to come over to Puddle. Tell the others.'

So presently in the Puddle High Street, where the natives were all scratching their heads and wondering what ailed their church clock, two large trucks pulled up and let loose a company of cameramen, prop hands, ballet chorus, and four dancers who were respectively to take the parts of the Student, the Girl, the Nightingale, and the Rose. Miss Tessa Porutska (née Prout), who was dancing the Nightingale, left her friends doing *battements* against the church wall and strolled along to Mrs Sherborne's, where she found Rodney having a conversation with Fred.

'But Fred,' he was typing, 'I have passed on to you every fact in my possession. Surely from what you have had you ought to be able to locate this banana-peel dropper?'

'Very sorry,' creaked Fred, 'the programming is

213

inadequate,' and he retired into an affronted silence.

'What's all this about banana-peel?' asked Tess, who was a very pretty girl, thin as a ribbon, with her brown hair tied in a knot.

Rodney explained that they needed to find a stagehand who had dropped a banana-peel on the stage at Covent Garden thirty years before.

'We'll have to advertise,' he said gloomily, 'and it may take months. It's not going to be as simple as I'd hoped.'

'Simple as pie,' corrected Tess. 'That'll be my Great-Uncle Toby. It was on account of him going on all the time about ballet when I was little that I took to a dancer's career.'

'Where does your Uncle Toby live?'

'Just up the street.'

Grabbing Rodney's hand she whisked him along the street to the forge where the surly Mr Prout, ignoring the ballet chorus who were rehearsing a Dorset schottische in the road just outside his forge and holding up the traffic to an uncommon degree, was fettling a set of shoes the size of barrel-hoops for a great grey brewer's drayhorse.

'Uncle Toby!' she said, and planted a kiss among his white whiskers.

'Well, Tess? What brings you back to Puddle, so grand and upstage as you are these days?'

'Uncle Toby, weren't you sorry about the banana-peel you dropped that was the cause of poor Rose Collard breaking her leg?'

'Sorry?' he growled. 'Sorry? Dang it, o' *course* I

was sorry. Sorrier about that than anything else I did in my whole life! Followed her up to London parts, I did, seeing she was sot to be a dancer; got a job shifting scenery so's to be near her; ate nowt but a banana for me dinner every day, so's not to miss watching her rehearse; and then the drabbited peel had to goo and fall out through a strent in me britches pocket when we was unloading all they unket rose-leaves on the stage, and the poor mawther had to goo and tread on it and bust her leg. Worst day's job I ever did, that were. Never had the heart to get wed, on account o' that gal, I didn't.'

'Well, but, Uncle Toby, did you ever *tell* her how sorry you were?'

'How could I, when she shut herself up a-grieving and a-laying curses right, left, and rat's ramble?'

'You could have written her a note?'

'Can't write. Never got no schooling,' said Mr Prout, and slammed down with his hammer on the horseshoe, scattering sparks all over.

'Here, leave that shoe, Uncle Toby, do, for goodness' sake, and come next door.'

Very unwilling and suspicious, Mr Prout allowed himself to be dragged, hammer and all, to the back of Rose Collard's garden wall. Here he flatly refused to climb over on Rodney's rope.

'Dang me if I goo over that willocky way,' he objected. 'I'll goo through the door, fittingly, or not at all.'

'But the door's stuck fast; hasn't been opened for thirty years.'

'Hammer'll soon take care of that,' said Uncle Toby, and burst it open with one powerful thump.

Inside the garden the nightingales were all asleep; sea-mist and silence lay among the thickets. But Uncle Toby soon broke the silence.

'Rose!' he bawled. 'Rosie! I be come to say I'm sorry.'

No answer.

'Rose! Are you in here, gal?'

Rodney and Tess looked at one another doubtfully. She held up a hand. Not far off, among the thickets, they heard a faint sound; it could have been somebody crying.

'*Rosie?* Confound it, gal, where are you?' And Uncle Toby stumped purposefully among the thickets.

'Suppose we go and wait at the pub?' suggested Tess. 'Look, the sun's coming out.'

An hour later Mr Prout came pushing Miss Collard's wheelchair along Puddle Fratrum's main street.

'We're a-going to get wed,' he told Rodney and Tess, who were drinking cider in the little front garden of the Haymakers' Arms. (It was not yet opening hours, but since the church clock now registered 5 a.m. and nobody could be sure of the correct time there had been a general agreement to waive all such fiddling rules for the moment.) 'A-going to get wed we are, Saturday's a fortnight. And now we're a-going to celebrate in cowslip wine and huckle-my-buff, and then my intended would like to watch a rehearsal.'

'What's huckle-my-buff?'

216

Huckle-my-buff, it seemed was beer, eggs, and brandy, all beaten together; Tess helped Mr Donn (who was another uncle) to prepare it.

The rehearsal was not so easily managed. When the chorus of village maidens and haymakers were halfway through their schottische, a runaway hay-truck, suffering from brake-fade, came careering down the steep hill from Puddle Porcorum and ran slap against the post office, spilling its load all the way up the village street. The dancers only escaped being buried in hay because of their uncommon agility, leaping out of the way in a variety of *jetés*, *caprioles*, and *pas de chamois*, and it was plain that no filming was going to be possible until the hay had somehow been swept, dusted, or vacuumed away from the cobbles, front gardens, doorsteps, and window-sills.

'Perhaps we could do a bit of filming in your garden, Miss Collard?' Rodney suggested hopefully. 'That would make a wonderful setting for the scene where the Nightingale sings all night with the thorn against her heart while Rose slowly becomes crimson.'

'I don't wish to seem disobliging,' said Miss Collard (who had watched the episode of the hay-truck with considerable interest and not a little pride; '*Well*,' she had murmured to her fiancé, 'just fancy my curse working as well as that, after all this time!'), 'but I should be really upset if anything – well, troublesome, was to happen in my garden.'

'But surely in that case – couldn't you just be so kind as to remove the curse?'

'Oh,' said Rose Collard, 'I'm afraid there's a bit of

217

a difficulty there.'

'What's that, Auntie Rose?' said Tess.

'As soon as you get engaged to be married you stop being a witch. Soon as you stop being a witch you lose the power to lift the curse.'

They gawped at her.

'That's awkward,' said Rodney at length. He turned to Tess. 'I don't suppose you have any talents in the witchcraft line, have you, lovey, by any chance?'

'Well, I did just have the rudiments,' she said sadly, 'but of course I lost them the minute I got engaged to you. How about Mrs Sherborne?'

'The curse has to be taken off by the one who put it on,' said Rose.

'Oh.' There was another long silence. 'Well,' said Rodney at length, 'maybe Fred will have some suggestion as to what's the best way to put on a ballet with a company of one-legged dancers.'

They drank down the last of their huckle-my-buff and went along to Mrs Sherborne's.

'Hello, Fred? Are you paying attention? We have a little problem for you.'

And that is why *The Nightingale and the Rose* was revived last year; it ran for a very successful season at Covent Garden danced by a company of one-legged computers, with Fred taking the part of the Nightingale.

One Foot on the Ground

by Jean Richardson

For years Moth Graham has lived and dreamed ballet and has wanted nothing more than to become a professional ballet dancer. Now she has reached a crucial stage in her training – an audition for a coveted place at the Royal Ballet School is looming …

'… And she was so busy fussing over Tom's chest that she forgot to ask about the party, so we didn't have to tell any lies after all.'

'But you'd told quite a lot in the first place,' Moth pointed out. 'Honestly, Libby, fancy saying that Gam knew all about the party and had said we could go. If I'd got back earlier and had to speak to Mrs B-S, it would all have come out, and I'd have been dragged in, and she'd be bound to have told Mummy.'

'Life is a risk,' said Libby, unimpressed. 'You don't achieve anything by staying at home and I'm glad I went. It was worth it just to see Hyde –'

'He sounds like some kind of tearaway. I don't know what you can see in someone like that.'

'Tastes differ. Some people can see things in precious stuck-up pianists –'

'Dan's not –' Moth, quick to come to Daniel's defence, blushed as she realized that Libby had noticed her interest.

Libby helped herself to another biscuit – there was only one left. 'Your turn to get the fish and chips, and then I suppose we'd better do some washing-up.'

'I'm so glad that Gam's coming home,' said Moth, relieved that Libby had changed the subject. 'It'll be marvellous to have real food again.'

There were, she had discovered, limits to her appetite for things on toast, things with chips, crispy pancake rolls (Libby's favourite) and even beef chop-suey.

◉

But although their great-aunt was determined to get back on her feet, she was declared housebound for the first few weeks and had to be content with hopping round on crutches. She had become, it seemed to Moth, smaller and frailer, as though the fracture had breached her defence against growing old; but her spirit was obstinately defiant.

'Thank you, but no,' she said firmly when the Health Visitor mentioned Meals on Wheels. 'They are for the elderly and handicapped. I still have all my faculties and two energetic nieces. I'm sure we can manage.'

And manage they did, though Libby grumbled at having to do the washing-up every evening and accused her great-aunt – though not in her hearing – of being too proud to accept help.

They were under pressure at school too, with the threat of O levels brandished at nearly every lesson and the approach of the all-important audition.

'Not that it'll do you any good,' said Miss Pearson briskly when Jane, who was unexpectedly in the final audition, brought a note from her parents asking for extra classes. 'You're not going to dazzle them with some sudden burst of talent you've picked up at the last minute. What they're looking for is long-term potential, qualities that will blossom under their special training and, above all, the right kind of physique. You've either got it or you haven't, and you'll be at your best if you just try and relax.'

Moth was tempted to ask Miss Pearson about her foot, which was increasingly painful after pointe-work, but she told herself that this was normal – surely she'd read of dancers bravely going on with bleeding toes. She would know soon enough anyway if something was seriously wrong because Marsha, who had auditioned the previous year and was now happily doing stage dancing, had told them what to expect.

'They divide you up into ... I think it was three groups – about twenty in each – and then you do a simple class. *Pliés*, *fondus*, *battements*, the usual sort of thing. And they watch you like hawks.'

'Who's "they"?'

'There were four of them; one was the principal and I suppose the others were teachers. They ask you to do frogs to show your turn out and they push your legs to see if the hip joint is free. That's all. I kept thinking how can my whole future depend on something so ordinary as a simple, everyday class.'

'And that's it?' In one of her favourite fantasies, Moth liked to see herself giving such an inspired display that she was offered a place on the spot.

'Well that's all I did.' Marsha would have liked to have made more of her story, and perhaps scare that spoilt Jane. 'We were asked to wait while they compared notes, and then they called out the names of those they wanted to stay on. I wasn't one of them, so I don't know what happened next.'

'I shall cry,' said Jane, who expected to be chosen, 'I know I shall cry if they don't call out my name.'

And sure enough she did.

◎

She was not the only one, though Moth was determined not to show her feelings. It had all been as Marsha said: a simple class taken by a brisk young teacher who gave them a brief reassuring smile before leading them into *pliés*, etc. Then they changed shoes for pointe work.

The studio with its mirrors and *barres* was like

all the others Moth had practised in over the years, and the other ... students they were called now, only a step away from the confident, purposeful adults who had jostled past them in the entrance hall, off to rehearse with Merle, Wayne, Julian, Marguerite ... the other students looked calm and serious, though inside they were probably as tense and nervous as Moth was.

'Wonder what they're saying?' said Tom, more to pass the time than because he expected an answer.

'They were writing things down,' said Libby, who had kept an eye on the auditioners. 'And they found us funny. Two of them were whispering – like we're not allowed to – and trying hard not to laugh.'

'I don't feel like laughing,' wailed Jane. 'I think I'm going to be sick.'

Tom, unhelpfully, suggested the fire-bucket, and the girls had just decided to go in search of the loo when one of the auditioners returned and they froze like statues.

The names were called alphabetically, so Tom came first.

'Tom Blundell-Smith.' He grinned with relief.

Everyone else seemed to begin with F ... Foster ... Forsyth ... Fraser ... Those at the end of the alphabet looked despairing.

'Elizabeth Graham.' Moth looked down. She would be next, if chosen ...

'Jennifer Graham.'

It was like musical chairs. She had survived for the moment, but only a handful of the last thirty would finally win.

◉

Moth knew on the way home that she hadn't made it. While Libby and Tom kept up their spirits by being rude about the other hopefuls, Moth was silent. It was no use pretending; she knew. Knew that she wouldn't be going to Talgarth Road, wouldn't

be learning the repertoire, covering rehearsals, waiting for the chance – because someone was suddenly sick or injured – that would magically put her on stage in the back row of the corps de ballet. None of that would happen. She wouldn't ever be a little swan – and she'd often linked hands with imaginary cygnets to that jaunty little tune – or ever dance at Covent Garden.

Her eyes pricked at the unfairness of it all: she had been deceived by dreams that had spurred her into practising, by teachers who had encouraged her when they ought to have known … Her anger and resentment became an anguish that made her feel sick. Noise, lights, movement stabbed at her head, yelling in triumph as they made her wince. Getting home seemed an almost impossible goal, and once there she went straight to her room and fell on the bed, burying her head beneath the welcome darkness of the pillow.

Libby told her worried great-aunt: 'Moth doesn't want any supper. She's got a bit of a headache.'

The pain was gone the next morning but Moth couldn't face going to school. What was the point? It was all over, everything she'd been aiming for all her life, and it no longer even seemed important. She lay there feeling numb, drained, remembering the hours she had spent practising, wondering how many classes she had done over the years ... She couldn't recall a time when she hadn't danced – and apparently it had all been for nothing.

When Libby breezed in to ask how she felt, Moth burrowed under the clothes and said she still felt sick ... not well enough to go today ... not well enough to go ever again, she wanted to say.

'OK, I'll tell Gam. Do you want anything – orange juice, cornflakes?' Libby thought she was shamming.

'No thanks.'

Later Moth heard the front door slam and felt relieved that Libby had gone. I shall take everything down, she thought, looking fretfully round the room. All those ridiculous reminders of being a dancer, they had betrayed her, fired her enthusiasm for a way of life that was now to be denied her. They had tempted and tantalized her, only to snatch away the prize as she had reached out for it.

She heard the downstairs clock strike the half hour and then the silence resumed. It felt unnatural to be doing nothing in the time that properly belonged to school. She pictured them in class, having a verb test, getting their history essays back

– she was sorry to miss that, as she was secretly proud of hers – but there was nothing there to tell her what to do with the rest of her life now that she couldn't dance.

She got up, pulled on jeans and a T-shirt, and unearthed an old sweater with frayed elbows. It felt comforting and don't-carish, though it didn't do anything for the cold deep inside her.

Her great-aunt was still in bed, but she heard Moth moving around and called to her.

Moth drifted into her bedroom.

'Libby said you weren't well. Are you feeling better?'

Moth shrugged her shoulders. 'S'pose so.'

Moth, who was incandescent when she was happy, drooped like a flower out of water. She's so transparent, her great-aunt thought, so easily cast down. She was afraid of saying the wrong thing, but she sensed Moth needed to talk.

'Tell me what happened yesterday. Did something go wrong?'

Moth's mouth trembled and she burst out: 'It's so unfair! Why let me go on dancing all this time if I haven't got the right kind of feet. Why didn't someone say so, ages ago?'

'Is that what the school said?'

'More or less. I was so pleased when I got through to the second round. I thought it was going to be all right. We had to do a few dance sequences and then we were examined by a doctor. He asked lots of questions and took lots of measurements, and then he looked at my feet and asked if I ever had any pain with them. My right foot does hurt sometimes, though I tried not to admit it, and then he said something about having a high extended instep. I asked him if that was bad, and he said that it would see me through life all right, but if I became a dancer I would be asking it to take a tremendous amount of strain, especially with pointe work, and I could end up crippled. He tried to explain but I didn't really take in what he was saying … I just knew that I wouldn't get a place … that it didn't matter how hard I'd worked …'

Moth was crying now as the pain freshened. 'I wouldn't have minded,' she sobbed, 'if I hadn't been good enough, if I hadn't worked hard, but this isn't my fault; it was all decided in advance – in a sense when I was born – and I never knew …'

She sat down on the bed and her great-aunt put her arms around her. 'Moth, dear, I'm so sorry. What a terrible disappointment, and how awful for you to find out like that.' She stroked Moth's hair gently and Moth inhaled a faint scent of far away flowers. 'No wonder you felt rotten last night. I wish I'd known. I hate to think of you going off to bed early by yourself. I wanted to come and see you, but I can't manage the stairs with those wretched crutches. What a pair we are: both wounded warriors.'

'I don't know what to do,' Moth confessed. 'I've never thought of becoming anything but a dancer. There really isn't anything else I want to be.

Honestly, Gam, I'm not just being difficult.'

'You feel that now, but you need time to adjust. Nobody knows what to do at first when they lose something important in their lives, but the answer will turn up, however impossible it seems now.'

'I know one thing: I'm not going back to school.'

'Well I don't suppose it'll matter for a few days. You may feel different next week.'

'I won't,' Moth said firmly. 'If I can't dance, then I don't want any more to do with dancing: no more classes, no more shows, nothing.'

Great-Aunt Marion didn't argue; she saw that Moth was in no mood to listen to reason, but Moth's mother was less understanding when she rang up that evening.

'Don't be silly, darling, of course you must go back to school. You must finish off the year at the Fortune, do your O levels, and then we can decide what to do next.'

'I want to go to another school.'

'All right, dear, but you can't change just now with the exams only two or three months away. Try and be sensible.'

'I'm not ever going to set foot in the Fortune again. I hate it. I hate all the teachers. It's their silly fault this has happened. They should have known about my feet ...' Moth dissolved into angry tears.

'Perhaps they should' – Mrs Graham was trying to appease Moth – 'but you are rather jumping to conclusions. After all, you haven't heard definitely that you haven't got a place.'

'I haven't, I haven't …' Moth shouted into the receiver. 'Don't be so stupid. They've got plenty of other girls to choose from, girls like Libby who've got the right kind of feet …' Libby … She couldn't bear to think of Libby being offered a place …

'We're not getting anywhere like this. You're obviously in one of your difficult moods. I'd like to have a word with Marion – I hope you're not taking it out on her.'

'No, I'm not, because she's not like you. She knows what dancing means to me and she can understand why I don't want to go to school …' Moth slammed the phone down and went off to her room as her great-aunt, looking concerned, hobbled into the hall.

Moth stuck to her decision not to go to school for the rest of the week. No one, not even Libby, said anything about it, and her great-aunt seemed positively to enjoy having Moth around the house. She did the shopping, some dusting and hoovering, and learned how to make pastry, surprising herself with a crisp steak and kidney pie that Libby, not one for flattery, pronounced terrific. It was as though she had had a severe illness – the kind children in old-fashioned books had – and was now convalescent. She knew that she couldn't go on like this, but she was grateful for the chance to recover in her own way.

Then one afternoon the bell rang, and there on the doorstep was Miss Pearson. Moth looked at her as though she belonged to another life.

'Well, aren't you going to ask me in? You won't come to me, so I thought perhaps Mahomet had

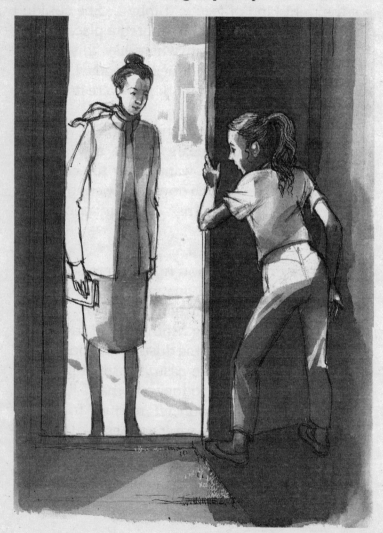

better come to the mountain.'

Moth grinned sheepishly. 'Did you want to see my great-aunt? She's lying down at the moment.'

'No, I've come to see you. I thought it might be easier to have a talk at home, where there's no one to disturb us.'

Moth led her upstairs and into the drawing room, where Miss Pearson perched on the settee and came straight to the point. 'I'm afraid the Royal Ballet school are not going to offer you a place because their osteopath feels that your feet aren't strong enough to take the strain of a career in classical ballet. I think you already knew that, didn't you?'

'Yes,' Moth agreed miserably. She had known, and yet ...

'I'm sorry, because I know you're disappointed and you're one of the most promising dancers we've had in a long time. Technique has never been your strong point – you feel too much to have a reliable technique – but you're blessed with an unusual creative appreciation of dancing.'

'The others ...?' Moth wanted to get it over.

'Tom has been offered a place and so has Libby. Linden has been accepted for the teaching course, but you weren't interested in that, were you?'

'No.' Moth couldn't stop the tears coming ... Libby who'd been her rival all along ... who was so unaffected by life and always got what she wanted ... Libby had fulfilled Moth's dream and would go on and on ...

Miss Pearson ignored Moth's tears. 'So what we

have to decide now is what you are going to do next, and I've got one idea you might like to consider.'

'I don't want to be a teacher or do my A levels and go to university,' Moth gulped. 'And I don't want anything more to do with dancing now that I can't dance.'

'Who said you can't dance?' Miss Pearson didn't sound in the least sympathetic. 'You can go on dancing if you're really determined, and I came round here because I thought that was what you wanted. I didn't know you'd changed your mind.'

'I haven't, but it's been changed for me, hasn't it?'

'My dear Moth, like hundreds of other aspiring dancers you've failed to get into a course that would have qualified you at best to be a classical dancer. What you think of as the lucky ones will get a training that will make them more marketable as classical dancers, but their chance of getting into the company is very remote. All the White Lodge students are put in one class and new recruits to the company usually come from that class; only the odd girl from the other classes stands a ghost of a chance of being picked. You certainly wouldn't have been, because you have neither the technique nor the temperament to stand up to the tough world of the company. Your gifts are only likely to flourish in very different soil.'

Moth didn't understand what she was getting at.

'The best thing you've done so far was that little ballet about the mad girl. You threw yourself into it because you enjoy creating, and I think that's the area we should concentrate on now.'

'But I can't just become a choreographer ...'

'No, of course not, but you stand a much greater chance of developing such a gift in a more fluid, experimental atmosphere, somewhere that welcomes ideas, that's closer to the way ballet is going in the future than a major prestige company can afford to be.'

'What sort of a place?'

'A friend of mine who teaches at a School of Contemporary Dance was impressed by your ballet and asked whether you'd thought of auditioning for them. I told her that you'd set your heart on trying for the Royal, and that you'd have to find out for yourself that you weren't right for them before you'd be prepared to consider anywhere else.'

'You knew all along that I wouldn't get in,' said Moth accusingly.

'I suspected it, yes, but it didn't seem a tragedy because I knew there were other things open to you.'

'But not the things I want. I quite like the contemporary dance classes, but not in preference to classical. I –'

'I suspect you don't really know much about it. You've been so set on one thing for so long that you've shut your eyes to everything else. If you'd ever seen the Martha Graham company or the London Contemporary Dance Theatre I don't think you'd feel I was suggesting some kind of second-class consolation prize. Contemporary dance isn't a poor second, Moth, it's an exciting challenge, and the school I had in mind has a teacher who trained with Graham and is the only person over here teaching the authentic Graham style. But if you don't want to know about it –'

'I do.' The world was right side up again. 'It's just that I thought I'd got to give up dancing ... and I've been trying not to think about it.'

'You give in very easily,' said Miss Pearson dryly. 'And I thought you were a fighter. There's no place in dancing for anyone who isn't. It's going to be disappointments and setbacks all the way, and you seem to have fallen at the first hurdle. Do you really want to go on?'

Moth didn't know. She'd heard all the talk about disappointments before, and battling against misfortune had always sounded so dramatic. But over the past week misfortune had left her numb and frightened, stumbling around in a paralysing web of depression. She couldn't any more, not with any conviction, say yes, I don't care what happens, I can take anything, because she wasn't sure that she could. But she did want to dance.

'Well, think it over.' Miss Pearson's tone was a shade more kindly in response to Moth's obvious distress. 'The auditions aren't until next term, so you've got time to find out about contemporary dance. Go and see the company if you can, and do some research into Martha Graham. They also have student programmes at the school, if you're interested.'

'If I do apply,' Moth said tentatively, 'would my feet be all right? I mean ...'

'Well I'm not a doctor, of course, and the audition will include a thorough medical examination, but I think the main objection to your feet was that the high arch wouldn't take the strain of continuous pointe work. Contemporary dance uses different techniques and no pointe work, so you should be all right.'

Moth wanted to hug Miss Pearson, and her delight showed.

'Moth, I'm not offering you a place at the school. I can't do that. If you do apply, you'll have to be prepared to be turned down again, you do understand that, don't you?'

Moth nodded.

'Good girl. Well I must be on my way. I've got a class at half past three and I mustn't be late. See you tomorrow – in class.' Moth didn't argue.

So Libby has passed, she thought as she came slowly up the stairs after Miss Pearson had gone. She knows where she's going for the next couple of years, whereas I ...

She heard her great-aunt calling from the bedroom.

'I dropped off and then I thought I heard the door bang. Is Libby home already? Is it time for tea?'

'No, not yet. I shut the door and I'm sorry I woke you up.' Moth didn't want to talk about Miss Pearson yet, not until she'd adjusted to her change of direction.

'Libby won't be home for another hour at least, so I thought I might go round to the library. Would you like me to change your book?'

'Please. I had a card this morning to say it's my turn for that new thriller and I'd love to settle down with a nice murder this evening.'

Moth smiled. Her great-aunt's voracious appetite for a good murder was a family joke. She took the card and bounced down the stairs, suddenly restless and tingling with energy. She had her own reason for going to the library: she wanted to see whether they had any books on Martha Graham – the name itself seemed a good omen – and contemporary dance.

Acknowledgements

The publishers are grateful to the following for permission to include material which is their copyright:

David Higham Associates on behalf of Bel Mooney for 'I Don't Want to Dance!' from *Prima Ballerina*, edited by Miriam Hodgson, published by Methuen Children's Books

A. M. Heath & Co. on behalf of Geraldine Kaye for 'Mega-Nuisance' from *The Spell Singer and Other Stories*, compiled by Beverley Mathias, published by Blackie in association with NLHC

Jean Ure for 'Hi There, Supermouse' by Jean Ure, published by Hutchinson

Harper*Collins*Publishers for 'The King and Us' by Jhanna N. Malcolm, published by Scholastic Inc.

Vivian French for 'Boys Don't Do Ballet – Do They?' by Vivian French, published by Kingfisher

Vanessa Hamilton on behalf of Margaret Mahy for 'The Hookywalker Dancers', published by J. M. Dent and Sons Ltd

Clarissa Cridland on behalf of Lorna Hill for *A Dream of Sadler's Wells*, published by Evans Brothers Ltd

Robert Chaundy on behalf of Jean Estoril for *Ballet for Drina*, published by William Collins Sons & Co. Ltd

HarperCollinsPublishers for *Come a Stranger* by Cynthia Voigt, published by William Collins Sons & Co. Ltd

A. M. Heath & Co. on behalf of Joan Aiken for 'The Rose of Puddle Fratrum' from *A Harp of Fishbones and Other Stories* by Joan Aiken, published by Jonathan Cape

Jean Richardson for *One Foot on the Ground* by Jean Richardson, published by Knight Books